The Days Of Jasper Caine

RICHARD EATON

Order this book online at www.trafford.com
or email orders@trafford.com

Most Trafford titles are also available at major online book retailers.

Printed in the United States of America.

ISBN: 978-1-4269-7397-0 (sc)
ISBN: 978-1-4269-7398-7 (hc)
ISBN: 978-1-4269-7414-4 (e)

Library of Congress Control Number: 2011910917

Trafford rev. 06/25/2011

www.trafford.com

North America & international
toll-free: 1 888 232 4444 (USA & Canada)
phone: 250 383 6864 • fax: 812 355 4082

Chapter One

Jasper Caine sprawled on the edge of the narrow ridge top and stared down into the canyon bottom that was now brightly lit by the early morning sun. The sun was not far up though and as yet it had done nothing to melt the frost that sparkled brightly on the grass and brush.

He was staring at two riders leading a pack mule that were coming up the trail that generally paralleled the small stream below. Jasper thought the little stream was Sims creek with the gulch named the same.

A shivering fit took him. He acknowledged that it had only partly to do with the frost that he lay on. "Dog--gone it." He swung and looked at Genevieve. "Dog--gone it, Genevieve, them there fellers acoming along is got to be trouble. I jus' know it."

Genevieve being used to Jaspers outbursts and grumblings said nothing back. Of course the fact that Genevieve said nothing probably had more to do with her being a horse, and so unable to talk, than mere disinterest. But on second thought, it would have been hard for her to project more disinterest than her head down, eyes closed posture would indicate.

Genevieve was a medium sized horse of an indeterminate brown color. When he'd `got' her, which even he had to admit was a euphemism for stealing her, she'd been quite skinny, with ribs being starkly visible under her skin. Good grass and light work had fattened her up considerably. When Jasper had started to put the pack saddle on her just after he `got' her, he couldn't take the skinny condition and the pitiful look she gave him, and so had ended up carrying the pack himself. On later moves after she'd gained some weight, he'd packed some of his gear on her. He had never had much to pack. He could easily do it himself, but he'd never got used to that pitiful look that she'd found out that if she gave him, she could always count on him packing most, if not all, his gear. Genevieve was far from a `dumb horse.'

Now, as he'd stared at the riders coming up the valley, Jasper had to wonder if they still hung horse thieves out here in the west.

Wondering about that, Jasper wanted to take it personally that Genevieve was not as concerned about this as he thought she should be. The trouble was, he thought he just didn't have the time right now. Finally he turned back to the canyon with a lot of inaudible grumbling in which the only thing that could be clearly heard was a couple of "Dog--gone."s

The riders were now no more than a couple of hundred yards down the river, although they were a couple of hundred feet lower in elevation. Jasper wasn't really worried that they'd hear him because he figured the murmur of the creek would mask what little noise he made. But he was worried now more than ever, because they were close enough to see that they wore the uniform of the forest ranger, or maybe game warden. He acknowledged to himself that he wouldn't know one from the other.

He heard Genevieve stomping around behind him, and without looking around, whispered, "Dog--gone it, Genevieve, be quiet." He heard the stomping hoof clomps taper off and he forgot about the horse as he gave his full attention to the two riders who were approaching the faint turn off trail that crossed the creek and moved up the small stream about a quarter of a mile before turning back into a small side canyon. That side canyon, if followed, turned back onto itself to head up nearly back to the canyon of the creek that it emptied into. The small pass between the side canyon head and the canyon it flowed into was where Jasper now lay.

He held his breath as they came to, and then passed the turnoff. It was unlikely that they'd see the trail that followed the other side of the creek now that they'd passed where it turned off. The reason it crossed the stream here instead of where it would enter the side canyon, was because of the high banks of the river that began where the trail crossed and continued for the most part of a mile. It could be crossed anywhere along that stretch and the banks were just very steep, not unclimbable, but without a reason to do so, he didn't figure they'd do it.

They seemed to not be concerned with anything that he could see. They just rode along as though they were intent on getting somewhere, only occasionally looking at the scenery they were passing through.

They were maybe a quarter mile up the stream and he was breathing much easier, when he saw something moving through the brush. It was on the opposite side of the creek from the two riders, which put it on his side. At first he thought it was an elk moving down to the creek, but it was moving straight at the two riders. He scratched his head, "Now that there's a mighty dumb elk." He muttered.

It crossed a small clearing that was only fifty feet from the edge of the stream. "That there's the strangest lookin elk I ever seen, I do believe. Why you know, Genevieve, I don't believe that theres an elk anyhow. It looks jus' like a horse." He mused on this for a minute. "Ya know, Genevieve, that there horse or elk, whichever, musta come outa this same leetle canyon what we're in. Right about there is where the canyon mouth is." He mused some more. Something was bothering him mightily about this whole thing.

It was right now that the horse, because it was now clear that that was what it was, slid down the bank and crossed the creek before climbing the other bank to the two riders. They'd seen the it coming and had stopped to sit and wait for it. Something about the way it went right up to them and then sidled around as though bashfully begging for a treat of some kind, was familiar.

Jasper sat for a moment trying to figure it out. Suddenly, he did, and it took his breath away. He snapped his head to the rear to check on what he was already sickly aware of. Genevieve was gone.

He slid back until he was far enough down to not be skylighted. He ran back until he could see down the dim trail they'd taken to get up here. No Genevieve. He dragged his hat off his head and threw it on the ground. Afterward still not satisfied, he began to leap up and down on it, hollering, although doing it quietly in deference to the proximity of the others, "Dog--gone it Genevieve. Now look what you gone and done." The hat had been a new baseball type hat with quilted ear flaps and in camouflage colors when this adventure started less than a month ago, but things going wrong had necessitated frequent stompings until now it was little more than a shapeless dusty rag.

Genevieve was a gregarious horse, and had somehow detected, maybe smelled, the other horses. Anyhow, there she was down with them there laws. Well, kind of laws. Like a lot of other things, Jasper was not at all clear of how much law power a forest ranger packed. No more did he know how much of the same law power a game warden was authorized to use. The only thing that he was sure of was that the others had passed close enough to see that they packed handguns, and one had a rifle racked in a saddle scabbard.

The fact that they had the firearms made him privately acknowledge that they had plenty of law power to do anything that they wanted out here in the wilds. His only option was to keep away from them.

Right now though, he had to see what was happening to Genevieve. He crawled back to the edge. The two riders were dismounted. One was petting Genevieve, and the other had crossed the creek and climbed the bank to look at the her back trail. Fortunately the trail here hugged the canyon edge and was a couple of hundred yards back from the stream. The uniformed man went only a short way along Genevieves back trail before the one that had stayed with the horses motioned him back.

They must have been going somewhere that had a schedule to it because just as soon as the other got back to the trail, they both mounted and hesitated only a short time, evidently discussing what to do about Genevieve. They must have decided to let her do what she wanted because they just turned on up the trail and let Genevieve stand. She could follow or go back to where she came from. It was clear from their actions that this was their decision. Genevieve hung back, standing and looking after them.

Jasper sighed thankfully. "Why shoot, she was justa wantin to socialize a leetle with them hosses. Now she done it, she'll come right on back." He told himself.

Genevieve looked up the trail after the men and then to the side into the side canyon that she'd come out of. She shook her head and then started to move up the trail after the departing riders. After a few feet she broke into a trot.

Jasper sadly gazed after her. "Dog--gone it, Genevieve. What for you leavin me? Them fellers won't treat ya right." He muttered. Feeling sorry for himself, he looked down at his hand. In spite of scrubbing it every chance he got, there seemed to be an ingrained dirt. He'd never imagined that camping out for weeks and months with no amenities that civilized people were used to could be so hard in some ways. Most of it he liked, but not the inability to have a hot shower. Many of the other things he'd always taken for granted were greatly missed also. Shaving for one thing. He'd often wished that he could just forget shaving when there was a choice about it. Now that he couldn't shave, he missed it.

He took stock of himself. He was about five foot eleven inches tall. When he'd come into the wilderness, he'd been a little chubby. Some unkind and jealous people that he'd known had even said he was fat. They'd never have known him now. Long hikes and missed meals had melted away any fat he'd ever had. The aforementioned beard was about an inch or so long and curly dark brown, which was curious as his hair had always been what he'd realistically described as dirty blond. What was more curious was that although his hair had not a smidgeon of grey, the darker beard was liberally streaked with it. No, he doubted that anyone that had known him would recognize him now.

It hadn't been a real great month since he'd entered the `Hiute Wilderness Area' in south central Colorado. This desertion and betrayal by Genevieve seemed to culminate a long series of misfortunes and broken hopes and strivings that had happened mostly during the past year.

He dropped his head to his folded arms and let his thoughts drift back. It had seemed that his misfortunes mostly dated from his losing his job at the bank a little more than a year ago. He'd be the first to admit that he'd never been one of the top bankers. His inclination had always been with the out of doors. He really couldn't have explained why he'd studied accounting in school. The fact that a girl he was very interested in had majored in the same thing, was a reason that he was careful not to examine too closely. The fact that once he got involved in it, his logical mind seemed to take to the discipline easily and almost of its own accord, might have been why.

Whatever the reason, after he graduated it had simply seemed easier to take the job he'd been trained for than to do anything else. By the time he figured out that he detested the job in the bank, it had seemed easier to just go along with it than to quit and do something that might have proved to be harder.

It wasn't that he had no initiative. He was very enthusiastic about spending his weekends and vacations in the out of doors. He spent all his spare time there and around outdoor people. It might have been in reaction to the surroundings of his working life that he'd began to mimick the folksy language of those he spent that spare time with and around. It must have been a gradual thing because the only unusual reaction to his slang filled talk was to those that he came in first time contact with. Those he worked with seemed unaware of it, so it must have been such a gradual thing that they'd been unaware of it happening.

The town he'd worked and spent his life in was in western New York. There was a fair amount of wilderness country around. It wasn't the kind of wilderness country that was to be found out here in the west. It was composed of low mountains, or maybe high hills, depending on your point of view. It was country that was in some ways just as wild as this country, but with centuries of use, with the last half century of very heavy use. But the only other point of view he had was that to be found in books and magazines, because as unusual as it may have been in this day and age of casual travel around the world, he'd never been further than one hundred and fifty miles from home in his life. At least until he'd headed out west just over a month ago.

Chapter Two

It had been just over two years ago that he'd met the girl that was destined to become his wife. He'd never really had much inclination to chase the women. Well, at least not since he had gotten out of school and discovered that he had a strong empathy with the wilderness. Oh, he'd gone with several, always taking them on hikes in the wilds to see how they stood up to it and whether they liked it. None had ever acted in a way that made him think they'd be compatible with his penchant for hiking and camping.

That had changed when he'd been hiking in the Delaware river area one Memorial Day weekend. He'd left the main trail with the vague idea of climbing a ridge that he thought might provide a good look at the surrounding country. He'd come around a bush in a small clearing with his entire attention focused on the ridge top.

He'd thought that he'd been paying close enough attention to the ground that he wouldn't stumble. The opposite proved to be true though. Someone had been sleeping in a sleeping bag and Jasper had walked right up and stumbled over them. That wasn't the worst though. On his way down he heard a muffled protest as he tried to catch himself by slamming his knee down. It was this knee slamming into the midriff of the one laying in the sleeping bag that had brought the protest. It was immediately ignored by Jasper though, as he fell full length across a smoldering campfire.

Without being aware of how he accomplished it at all, he seemed to levitate himself from the fire and throw himself backwards away from it. In doing so, he landed full length on the person in the sleeping bag. The gasping protests had never quit, and with this new assault, they doubled in intensity.

Jasper was so befuddled by these events that he just lay there trying to collect his wits. Suddenly, whoever was in the sleeping bag and under him must have figured that enough was enough. Legs and arms pistoned upward and propelled Jasper into the air again. The trouble was that by chance he was propelled back to where he'd just succeeded in escaping: namely the fire. This time he landed face down in it and immediately he smelled his hair begin to scorch. With a loud squawk, he rolled out and began to beat himself about the head just in case his hair was on fire. It turned out that it wasn't. It also turned out that he'd rolled the right way that time and landed on the opposite side of the fire from the girl that was emerging from the sleeping bag with fire in her eye.

"Fool." She screamed at him. Her mouth worked trying for a suitable epitaph, which she obviously intended to bestow on him posthumously. Her anger overcoming her ability to dredge a suitably low description, she screamed, "Oh...." And grabbing a branch that had been intended for the fire, she ran around it, clearly intending bodily harm. Jasper, who had just now begun to gather his wits about him again, was nevertheless smart enough to see that where he was, wasn't a healthy place. He ran the other way.

After a couple of circles of the fire the girl stopped and regarded him with a crafty look. That fire wasn't near big enough to stop a determined woman and Jasper, while not the smartest man in the world, at least wasn't that dumb. He departed for the far tree line. He must have been a good runner because just before he got to the trees, the girl began to holler again. Peeking over his shoulder at her, he saw that she'd stopped and was standing and brandishing the limb while challenging him to be a man and stand and fight. He thought that some of the things she called him was right down scandalous. But not, of course, scandalous enough to stop to complain.

Once into the trees, he stopped and listened to see if she'd follow. Except for occasional renewed bouts of abuse that grew fainter as she obviously withdrew to the fire, he heard nothing more of her. He sat down on a handy log and took stock of himself. He discovered several scorched and lacerated places on various portions of his body. These he paid small attention. He sat and stared toward the edge of the clearing. He couldn't see it from here, but he wasn't looking at it anyhow. In his mind, he could see the girl. He wasn't sure how he was seeing her because all he'd been aware of when they'd been in the meadow was trying to keep from being hit on the head with a branch. But just sitting here, the picture of her came clearly.

He thought her height would probably be about four inches shorter than his. That'd make her about five six or seven maybe. A nice height, he thought happily. A full head of tousled brownish blond hair. Just about the color of mine, he mused. She'd been wearing a sloppy sweater, that while it drooped, did little to hide a lithe slender body. A pair of faded blue jeans completed her attire. She'd been wearing no foot wear, probably because she'd been in her sleeping bag. Thinking about it, he decided that the fact that she'd been wearing no shoes might have been all that saved him. He idly wondered how fast she'd have moved with shoes and if she'd have done more than just threaten him with the branch.

He was startled to realize that he wanted to see more of her. When she'd been chasing him, all he'd wanted to do was get far away.

Now he got up and moved slowly back toward the clearing edge. As the clearing showed up as a thinning of the foliage ahead, he moved laterally until he found a bush thick enough to hide him but still let him see.

She was hunkered at the edge of the fire building it up. Periodically, she'd turn and grumble something. He was too far to hear clearly but he figured that was to the good under the circumstances. After a while it seemed that she forgot him, as she didn't turn anymore.

He gave it a while longer before moving quietly out a little way into the clearing. He poised himself for flight before calling hesitantly, "Uh..ma'am."

He flinched back as she whirled. But she didn't do anything more than glare at him, at least for now, although he noted that the branch was near to her hand. "Uh ma'am. I just want to apologize for....." He hadn't thought this out before. What did he want to apologize for. The truth was, he just wasn't at all sure of what had happened. He'd been walking along looking up at the ridge, and then things had seemed to happen in a blur. He noticed her eyes were blue. A blazing kind of blue, it seemed right now.

The tightly reined in anger seemed to seep over a little. She grabbed the branch and straightened as she turned. "What did you attack me for?" She had a rather low husky voice, even though it was now strained with anger.

"Well ma'am, you see, what I was a doin', I was walkin along lookin at that ridge right there." He gestured behind him. "I guess I musta tripped over you and I guess I landed in your fire. After that, things seemed to get kind of excited. I don't really know what happened, but I sure do apologize." He thought her lips would be appealingly full if they hadn't been set in a hard straight line.

"Oh, looking at the ridge huh? Fell in the fire huh?" She brandished the branch.

"Well, jus' look here." He pulled his cap off to show singed hair. Turning his head, he showed the laceration where he'd landed on something. It was still seeping a little blood. He was gratified to see something shift in her eyes. Her lips relaxed a little. He was right about them too.

"Is that really what happened? How could you trip over me in broad daylight this way?" She looked at the sun that indicated near noon, as though to say how could anyone be so clumbsy.

He shrugged wryly, "Might be thats the reason. I guess I didn't expect anyone to be sleepin' this time of day."

Her expression darkened again, and he hurried on, "Mind, that's not an excuse. I jus' wasn't lookin' where I was goin. I hope you're not hurt any?" He made it a question.

At the reminder, her free hand came up to her right shoulder and absently massaged it. "Well, I guess I came up with a bruise or two.

Nothing permanent, I guess. As to why I was sleeping, I hiked in from Stantons' Landing last night. Only got here about four o'clock. Guess I was tired. I usually don't sleep this long even if I am tired, though." She shrugged.

He looked at her with respect. "Stantons' Landing?" He considered. "Why, that's gotta be twenty miles, don't it?"

She glanced around her as though she wasn't precisely sure where she was. That was probably correct if she'd got here in the dark. Jasper had been over this country several times and he couldn't have put a precise distance to it. "Well, I'd say it might be closer to twenty five miles, although I couldn't swear to it."

Jasper moved closer. "Ma'am, I've gotta say that thats hikin. An in the dark too." His admiration was evident.

She hefted the branch slightly at his approach. Then as if deciding that he had to be harmless, she let it sag to the ground. "Well, I've never been afraid of the dark. Besides, I've only got two days off. I have to make the most of it when I can."

Jasper stared at her. "You like the wilds enough to hike all night to get into it? You do this often?"

"Yes to both. I try to get away from the plastic civilization when ever I can." As if she finally had lost all her anger and suspicion, she gestured at the fire. "Guess it's breakfast time. Set down and I'll see what I've got."

He couldn't take his eyes off her face as he moved around the fire. Because of that, he didn't see her pack and he walked right over it. It fell over, spilling most of what it contained into the dirt. Scooting around to pick it up, he knocked over her large canteen. It didn't have the cap on and water commenced to gurgle out. Turning to pick it up, he stepped right in the middle of the carton of eggs that had spilled from the pack.

She darted forward to rescue them, dismay written on her face. She arrived just at the same time he turned and bent to try to pick up what was left. Their heads met with a crack that was hard enough to make them both set down hard on the ground.

He waited for another explosion, and was greatly relieved when after just a moment, he was greeted with a rueful giggle. And then roaring laughter, in which after a short hesitation, he gratefully joined in. In the end they were able to salvage four eggs for breakfast.

This was the start. At the end of the breakfast, it seemed that they knew enough about each other to carry things on. It turned out that she lived only forty miles from Jaspers home town. Four months later, they were married.

Chapter Three

At first, the love they shared for the outdoors seemed to be enough. Mostly, June, for that had turned out to be her name, ignored the fact that Jasper seemed to be one of the truly accident prone people. It seemed to be helped along by the fact that he spent half his time in a seeming daze, dreaming of getting away into the wilderness. She shared this inclination. In some ways she was even more enthusiastic to get away from people than he was.

The third time that he in some way got the table cloth caught on his belt, and pulled it and most of the table ware off onto the floor, she could manage no more than to keep quiet as she stalked off into the bedroom and slammed the door.

After he'd cleaned up the mess, she came out and apologized for her moodiness. But it just got worse. In spite of his love for her, which was strong enough to cause physical sickness when he pulled one of his stupid stunts, he just couldn't seem to help it. When they were newly married, she'd seemed to think that he was doing most of the clunky things that happened just to keep her amused, and that they would stop when he wanted them to. With the knowledge that it was not within his power to do anything but what seemed natural to him, the appreciation waned to eventual outright hostility when accidents happened.

Looking back now, he thought it was probably the nervousness caused by the growing insecurity of his marriage that had proved to be the thing that cost him his job. On the job was the one place that his accident prone nature had seemed to keep its distance. Oh, some things happened, but he'd always thought that the concentration that the job demanded kept him on the straight and narrow there.

That began to change. Things began to go wrong. He'd go to the water cooler for a drink and somehow his coat would catch on the cooler and as he walked away, the cooler would come too, nearly drowning those close by. No really important things, and most were amused at first. But as with his wife, over a period of time the amusement turned to outright hostility. In spite of, or maybe because of, his earnest striving to improve himself in this regard, things just seemed to get worse.

He wasn't aware that things were any worse than usual when he was summoned to the managers office. Thinking about it later, he figured it was just a cumulative thing. They had simply had enough.

After that he'd had a series of jobs. His accident prone nature seemed to have gotten worse though. Probably through his loss of any confidence whatever in himself. There was no problem with money at first. Not a real problem even at the last. He'd always saved quite a bit of his pay. His hobbies of the outdoors had never been the type that had cost much. Once he'd got the basics of pack and associated gear, he spent very little on his outings. He had enough money saved that they could have lived for a year at their present level.

Over the months, the conversation between Jasper and June seemed to become more and more strained. This caused him almost more pain than he could bear. And it seemed that the harder he tried, the more outrageous things seemed to go wrong. He guessed that June tried even harder than he did, but it was something that was beyond her will. She became more withdrawn as time went by.

Just about two months ago, he'd come in from hunting for a new job, the last one being a job of hauling two by fours on a construction job. He'd managed to nearly bury himself and one other laborer when he tried to take a board from near the bottom.

He'd had no luck that day and when he walked in the front door, he'd known. Maybe it was the stillness. He tried a hesitant "June" that seemed to be swallowed by the silence. He walked hesitantly into the front room. The dining table was clean and bare except for the note that was neatly centered there.

It said. `Jasper. I'll have to take the blame for this. You've done what you could and I know that. But I can't take it any more. I'm leaving before I destroy us both.' It was signed `June' he walked to the sofa on legs that felt like sticks. After he'd sat down it seemed to be more than he could take and in the way the brain has of taking care of insupportable pain, it simply turned him off.

It was pitch black when he came to himself again. He turned his head to the clock. The brightly lighted digital numbers told him it was eight minutes after three. After sitting and staring at it for a while, he got up and went into the bedroom. He threw a couple of changes of cloths into his pack on top of his usual camping equipment that was always left packed there. When he left the house, he didn't even close the front door.

He opened the door of the ancient pickup that was the only vehicle he'd ever owned. Before getting in, he stood and surveyed the house thinking. There was no one he needed to notify. His parents had been killed in a head on car wreck three years ago. The only other living relation that he knew of was an aunt in california some where. They'd never corresponded and he had no real idea of where she was. He had an idea that she wouldn't welcome hearing from him anyway. Somehow though, the idea of seeing his only relation appealed to him. He had an errant thought that maybe he would try and find her someday. Just maybe that was why he pulled out of town that early morning heading west. He had no other conscious reason for doing so.

He'd driven until sunup. With the growing light, his exhaustion deepened. He wasn't sure whether he'd actually slept last night, but now his eyes burned until he couldn't see. He pulled over to the side of the road and got out to walk around and get some air. When he got back in the pickup it seemed the most natural thing in the world to just lie down in the seat and sink into deep dark sleep.

It was the middle of the afternoon when he woke up. After walking around and limbering up, he was able to think a little more logically. He didn't have much money. He had a couple of hundred dollars in his checking account. He decided that he needed it if he was going anywhere. There was a couple of thousand more in a certificates of deposit with a savings and loan company. He'd have to go back and spend the time necessary if he was to get that. Although he would regret it in the future, right now the last thing he could have stood for would have been to go back and do the things necessary to get that money. He made up his mind not to think of it anymore. He'd try to get his money in the checking account and let that be enough. He hoped he wouldn't have to retrace his path all the way back to his home town. In the end he decided to go on down the road. See if he could cash a check in the next town.

That turned out to be only about ten miles. It proved to be a small town that nonetheless boasted several banks, one of which was the same bank that held his account. He had no trouble closing it.

After that, he kept moving for several days, or maybe weeks. He'd never be sure of the exact amount of time. He'd drive as long as he felt like it, or until he saw some place he wanted to spend a little time. These places were all wilderness areas of one kind or another. Some days he drove no more than fifty or sixty miles. Some days he drove none at all, just sitting or hiking as the notion moved him. His direction was always west. But he tended to drift a little south too, so that when he entered Colorado an indeterminent number of days later, it was on highway Fifty in the east central part of the state. It was as he was pulling into the town of La Junta that he began to hear an ominous noise. It was a tapping sound, but try as he would, he couldn't isolate it to any one part of the engine.

Stopping at a service station that advertized a full time mechanic, he was told to pull it in to the hydraulic lift. He idled away about two hours by strolling up the street. It was then that he spotted the buckskin shirt in the shop window. The price was forty five dollars. He counted his money. The only expenses he'd incurred on the trip was for gasoline and food. It turned out that he had just under a hundred dollars left. He shook his head and walked away. He had a long way to go and as it was he'd have to find a job of some kind before long.

When he got back to the service station he was met by the mechanic, who gave him the news. What he'd heard tapping was a connecting rod. Not really surprising in a truck this ancient, the mechanic allowed. How much to fix it? Asked Jasper. After several minutes of scratching his head and muttering, most of which seemed to be concerned with how hard it would be to find parts for something that old, he came up with the figure of eight hundred fifty dollars.

Jasper waited for him to start laughing. This had to be a joke. The whole pickup hadn't cost him that much when he'd bought it. The other simply stood and stolidly regarded him. "Eight fifty? You mean that thing will cost eight fifty to fix?"

The other turned and solemnly regarded the pickup for a moment before turning back and answering, "Yeah, I figure that eight fifties the minimum. Depends on how hard it is to find parts. Could be more."

Jasper stared at him. It seemed that life was determined to play jokes on him no matter what. He shook his head. Without a word, he moved up to the pickup and took his pack out of it. Checking inside the cab for anything else that he wanted, he hoisted it his shoulders and moved off to the street.

The mechanic had been watching him curiously. Now as Jasper moved off, he asked what to do with the pickup. Jasper ignored him. At last he seemed to realize that Jasper was just leaving, and he followed a short way, hollering and screaming about what to do with the pickup. Jasper didn't look back.

When he got to the shop that had the buckskin shirt, he went in and bought it.

It was evening when he got to the west end of town. He had a vague idea of hitch hiking on west, but at the sight of a cafe, he realized how hungry he was. He went in and took a booth. While he was waiting for service, he began to idly read a placemat that was on the table. It was devoted to detailing the attractions of Colorado in a large scale way.

It was then that he first saw a reference to the Hiute wilderness area. He saw in the small print in one corner that further information about any area of the map was available at the cashiers counter. He went up and paid fifty cents for a four page booklet extolling the attractions of the Hiute area along with directions to campgrounds that had parking lots for the wilderness area hikers. Motor driven vehicles were prohibited in the area itself. He studied the tract as he ate.

Looking back, he really didn't think he'd made up his mind to anything when he walked out of the cafe. He'd been mightily impressed by the descriptions of Hiute area, but he hadn't thought of going there right now. It seemed he just had too many problems. He had, in fact, started for the highway to start hitchhiking. He had to detour around a one horse trailer parked to the side of the cafe. He didn't realize there was a horse in it until a nose poked out through a crack in the side. The trailer was rather decrepit, as was the pickup that it was hitched to, now he noticed it.

He rubbed the horses nose. He wished he had something to feed it. He'd never had a chance to ride a horse before. Oh, there were places that horses could be rented back where he came from, but he'd always been too busy to take the time. He'd certainly entertained no thoughts of having a horse out here. And truth be told, he didn't now.

Again reflecting on it, he truly couldn't have said what made him move around the pickup to the drivers side and look at the ignition. Just like it had been set up, the keys dangled from the lock. Without any hesitation, he crawled in and started the vehicle. He looked back as he drove away. No one was in sight, and he never saw any sign of pursuit. At eleven o'clock that night, he turned the pickup west on a gravel road that eleven miles later, stopped at a large campground on the east edge of the Hiute wilderness area.

Chapter Four

He slept the rest of the night in the pickup after unloading the horse and tying her where she could get grass and water at the small creek.

He lost no time the next morning in putting an old pack saddle that he found in the trailer on her. It was when he started to tie the pack to the saddle with some rope that he found in the trailer, that he saw how thin she was. Petting her and apologizing for even thinking of making her pack his things, he put the pack on his own shoulders and taking the twenty two rifle that hung from a window rack in the rear window, he moved up the trail leading the horse.

He stayed on the trail for about ten miles before turning off along a small creek bed. He kept going for several more miles before turning off up a side canyon. On a grassy bench a couple of miles up, he made camp and stayed for a couple of weeks while he scouted his back trail for pursuit. From all he'd seen, at least until this morning, it might have been that they'd never even found the pickup and trailer where he'd abandoned them.

For all his bumbling nature, he was skillful and experienced in the wild. He'd brought no food with him at all, but he had no trouble feeding himself. He knew what plants were good to eat, and although it was still early spring here in the Colorado mountains, the sun on the south side of ridges had sprouted much that was good to eat. Although jasper got tired of some of the things he ate, he never went hungry. He also got a rabbit with the twenty two from time to time. He could have killed a number of deer, but he knew that he'd have wasted a good part of the meat and that was something he was unwilling to do.

After a couple of weeks, he felt more secure and began to move around more. He spent several days following the trails here and there, finding where they led and how they were situated. He figured it was necessary information in case someone did come hunting him and he had to move quickly.

Coming into the wilderness area had done little to cure his bumbling nature. One morning looking over his shoulder and talking to Genevieve, he'd fallen over a log that he'd failed to see and sprawled full length into a patch of poison ivy. There'd been several similar happening too. There wasn't anyone up here to see the things he did though, except Genevieve, and though she looked at him at times as though she thought he was crazy, he didn't mind the things that happened nearly as bad as he had in civilization.

He'd found this bench about a week ago. He liked it because of how it was situated, overlooking the trail below. He could keep track of anyone using it without exposing himself. The fact was though that this was a minor side trail and the travelers this morning were the first that he'd seen.

This brought him to now. He raised his head and turned his eyes to the trail. Maybe Genevieve had decided to return. But all that was in sight was a stretch of empty trail that seemed to mock him.

All at once, from out of nowhere came anger. It seemed that he couldn't take rejection again, at least not right now. He knew that Genevieve was just a horse and not really responsible for leaving him. If he got her back, she'd be alright. She'd got attached to him while they were together and he'd come to think of her as much more than a horse. In fact, right now, she was all the family he had or was likely to have.

He sat up. The anger turned to determination. He wasn't going to just sit and let Genevieve go. He'd follow them and get her back, thats what he'd do.

He'd started down the trail when something occurred to him. He stood and considered. He knew the trail the others had taken because he'd followed along it before settling down where he was. It went north for about five miles before rounding a point of the mountain. Then it returned south again on the other side. He thought that where the trail was situated directly opposite the mountain to the east was probably not more than a couple of miles distant. That meant that while the laws would have to go ten or more miles, he could get to the same place by going two. The fact that the two miles facing him were mostly either straight up and down, or at least extremely steep going simply made him determined to hurry and get at it.

He set off up the mountain. When he'd come into the mountains here, although he'd been somewhat overweight, that in itself was somewhat deceptive. He'd always been a hiker, as heretofore told, and hiking had always kept him in at least fairly hard condition. The last month had put him in a lean and firm condition that made short and easy work of the uphill part of the trip. He hit a couple of areas of cliff that he had to detour around, but the detours were small and he was held back very little and didn't lose much time.

On top, there was a short distance of more or less level ground before the slope pitched precipitously down. The downhill part of the hike was much more difficult to control than the uphill part. It made for slower going, so as not to make a misstep that would send him down the mountain in an uncontrollable slide. Even allowing for that, he made pretty good time for most of the way down.

It was about two thirds of the way to the bottom that he came on a stretch of cliffs that seemed to extend a long way each direction. He was about in the center of where the cliffs curved in a kind of shallow u shape and went as far as he could see both ways. They seemed to be of a consistent height from where he stood to the fartherest reaches. As far as he could tell, that was about one hundred feet.

He stood considering. There was too much foliage in the way to see the trail that he knew ran along the bottom of the canyon here. He could see glints of water through the trees and bushes here and there, and from that he figured it was no more than a quarter of mile on down.

There were some thick and strong trees growing here close to the top of the cliff and he decided that the thing to do was loop his rope around one of the trees and let himself down. Anything else would have him detouring so far that he was worried that he'd get down to the trail after the riders passed.

The only thing that worried him was his rope was less than two hundred feet long and it might not be long enough to get him to the bottom. He'd have to loop it so that when he got to the bottom, he could let go of one end and pull the rope up around the tree and down to be recovered. He thought that he'd be within a few feet of the bottom when he got to the end of the rope and he'd be able to jump on down.

Without any further thought, he looped the rope around the tree and let himself over the side. Going down the cliff wasn't all that hard. He just walked down, more less, as he let the rope slide around his waist and controlled his descent with his hands. He was feeling pretty proud of himself when all at once he felt the knots in the end of his rope hit his hand. This was the upper hand and the rope ran through it and then around his waist before feeding through his other hand. By clamping his hands, he was easily able to hang there while he decided how he was going to get down the remaining thirty feet. It was hard to believe that he'd miscalculated this badly.

Well, he sure couldn't jump thirty feet without the danger of breaking something. There wasn't anything to do but climb back up and make the detour. This was going to make him late getting to the trail, of that he was nearly sure.

Sighing, he let go with one hand to take a new hold on the rope and haul himself up. For a split second, he hung there disbelieving that he'd let go with the wrong hand. He'd meant to let go with the hand that held just one of the pieces of rope, the hand that held the other would have been able to easily hold him until he got another hold to climb, but he'd let go with the wrong hand and the rope whipped around him and out of his hand. He was falling free. He screamed "Dog--gone it." It seemed to come out as an immensely loud screeching bellow at the injustice that always seemed to inhabit his world.

Directly beneath Jasper grew a large scrub oak brush. It was thick and strong, and when he hit directly dead center, it scratched and mauled him. It also slowed his fall somewhat. He emerged from the bottom side of the bush like a quick spit prune pit. Right at the bottom of the bush, a small arroyo began. It was cut into the shale that was the stuff of the mountain right here. The arroyo bottom was of weathered shale that were mostly of marble sized pieces. It was very steep here, being probably seventy or eighty degrees. The steep arroyo with its small pieces of shale seemed to act like ball bearings to speed his journey down the mountain. In fact, he seemed to pick up speed rather than slow down. This precipitous ride lasted for some two hundred yards.

At this point, the slope began to level out a bit, and it was here that bushes began to occur in the bottom of the arroyo. Jasper hit the first like a giant bowling ball. And like a bowling ball, he simply uprooted the bush although it slowed him slightly. At the jar of the bush, Jasper squalled again, a high piercing screech. The slope seemed to level out more in a short time and more bushes were there. Jasper didn't tear these bushes out by the roots, but he tore through them and each one slowed him more until he finally hit a more or less solid wall of them that finally stopped him.

He lay there for a few minutes trying to figure out how bad he was hurt. He seemed to ache and smart all over, but none of the aches seemed to be too bad right now. Finally, he moved enough to feel himself and take stock. To his amazement, there seemed to be little wrong with him. His heavy denim pants were abraded here and there, but he only found a little blood on one place on his leg. Further exploration revealed that it was only scratched. The buckskin shirt had seemed to protect his upper body very well.

He lay there a little longer, but just as he decided that he was alright and made a small move to get up, a sound made him freeze to immobility again.

A horseman moved into sight about twenty feet away. The bushes were thick enough that he was sure that as long as he lay still, he'd be safe from the others discovery. He could see good enough though, to tell that it was one of the men that he'd seen this morning. The man stopped at that point. The other horseman must have been a little way back, because the one he could see turned and looked behind him to talk. "I tell ya Jake, that there mountain lion that we heard asquallin' should be right about here somewhere."

"Dang Sam, I do wish you'd quit a lallygaggin'. We gotta git on about our business. I don' believe that was a mountain lion nohow. Sounded like a sick eagle to me." This from the hidden man. He sounded older than the rather young man that Jasper could see.

The first man snorted. "A sick eagle?" He asked disgustedly. "I say that was a lion asquallin'." He seemed to consider a moment. "Course, that there lion didn't sound just right. I think maybe somethin' mighta been wrong with him." He considered again before declaring. "I think that there lion was prob'ly jus' a little off his feed. Constipated or somepin." He finished decisively.

Jasper moved his head up slightly to glare at the man. He wished that he dared to tell him what he thought of that opinion, but he kept quiet with an effort.

"Well, whatever it was, it ain't gonna tell us nothin else. Le's git on about our business."

The other still looked dissatisfied with all of it, but he grunted an assent and moved on out of sight. The older man came into sight for a moment as he moved on. Just as Jasper started to move, Genevieve walked into sight. She hesitated and turned her head to look in his direction. He didn't know whether to hope she would remain or not. At this point, the rangers or gamewardens, whichever they were, would probably come back to see what had happened to her. He needn't have worried, after a short hesitation, she moved on after them.

Chapter Five

When he could no longer hear anything at all of their passage, Jasper climbed to his feet, untangling himself from the thick brush as he did. A couple of sharp twinges made him gasp and hesitate until they felt better, but when he finally reached his feet and stood upright, he felt surprisingly good.

He moved cautiously to the edge of the trail and looked after them. The foliage down here in the bottom was uniformly thick and the trail took a bend after about a hundred yards that effectively hid anything past it. Glancing down, he saw that the only fresh tracks were the ones of the party he was after. He should have little trouble trailing them.

After a half mile, he stopped and took stock of himself. He was surprised to find that he was comfortable. The slight aches and stiffened muscles had taken very little time to work themselves out. He felt strong and good, able to go on after genevieve whatever it took.

The trail followed the river along for about four or five miles before the river merged with a larger stream and the trail merged with the larger trail that followed it. The trail of the two men turned up it and Jasper followed along.

Within the space of a couple of miles, the river bottom narrowed and at the places the river swung close to the side of the bottom of the steep mountain slope, the trail, of necessity, climbed and switchbacked up various distances before dropping to the river level again. At first, he still felt strong and tackled the trail up and down without really thinking about it.

Four hours later and in the middle of the afternoon, he wasn't so sure. Counting the twists and turns of the trail, not to mention all the ups and downs, Jasper thought that he might have trailed them the most part of twenty miles. Bruises that had felt insignificant this morning after his slide down the hill and the first short walk after, now made their presence known in a sharp complaining manner. He was taking short rests much more often and was worried that the others were getting too far ahead.

An hour later though, he came over a ridge and saw the horses on a small meadow about a quarter of a mile ahead.

Dropping quickly behind some small bushes to the side of the trail, he looked for any sign that he'd been seen. The fact was that the two men were nowhere in sight. Their two mounts and the pack mule were tethered to a bush on long ropes that allowed them to graze. Genevieve was loose but kept to the close proximity of the other horses.

Laying still felt good and he had the excuse of not wanting to move until he knew the whereabouts of the two men. By the time he'd been here for another half hour and was beginning to cast worried looks at the sun that now was less than an hour from dropping behind the western peaks, the waiting was far less than satisfactory. A few minutes later, he was glad to see the two come onto the far side of the meadow. There was a middling size side canyon over there with a small creek tumbling down over large boulders. They'd obviously been up the canyon for some reason. Their reasons for being up there seemed to be far less important to Jasper than what they intended to do now.

When they got to the horses, they stood for a while discussing something. The younger made frequent turns, pointing here and there with exaggerated arm swings and body movement. The older of the two was far less demonstrative, but seemed to be holding up his end of the argument. He must have been for stopping here, because after five or ten minutes of this, the younger one threw up his hands and began to unsaddle the stock.

After a short scout around the area, the older of the two gestured to a grove of trees at the far side of the meadow and each grabbed a pack box and moved off that way. They returned and stacked the saddles under a tree. Taking their bed rolls, they moved off to the grove to set up camp.

The meadow was a pretty stretch of grass, bordered on one side by the stream that emerged from the side canyon the two had been up. The main canyon with the trail that Jasper was following had a larger stream that formed the border on the side closest to him. The larger stream had carved a stream bed that was some fifty yards across and with thick brush in the fairly level bottom. The meadow was across the main stream bed from jasper.

The two men were setting up their camp deep enough in the grove of trees that they were entirely hidden from Jasper. He thought that they'd even be hidden from the meadow. Casting a worried glance at the sun that was no more than a hands breadth from the western ridgeline, he moved off toward the meadow, although being careful to keep to the cover of the trailside brush.

Trying to move quietly through thick brush was a time consuming business and by the time he'd reached the river, the sun had gone completely. There was still plenty of light to see what he was doing though. He moved across a shallow place easily enough, although getting wet half way to his knees. A few minutes later, he moved cautiously up over the four foot high bank that separated the meadow from the lower river bottom.

The horses were about one hundred and fifty feet out on the meadow and he crouched looking around before he stood up and quietly called to Genevieve. She threw her head up and saw him. Snorting joyfully, she trotted over and nosed him. He'd picked a handful of grass to give her, which he now did. She picked it politely from his hand as she always did and then playfully nosed his pockets for more.

Jasper was so gratified to have his arms around her neck that he'd temporarily forgotten the two men. He was unpleasantly startled to hear one of them talking as he came closer. Snapping his head that way, he saw movement in the edge of the trees where they'd camped. One of them, or maybe both were coming. He didn't think they'd seen him, it was probably just Genevieve snorting that had made them decide to investigate. But what ever the circumstances, he had only seconds to get under cover where they wouldn't see him.

He was completely in the open here. His only chance was to get down into the river bottom where he knew the thick brush would hide him. The edge of the bank that he'd come over was only a dozen feet behind, and taking a run, he jumped over. The light had gone until the brush in the bottom was rendered rather indistinct and he just jumped full length to crash through some sage brush and land face down in the dust and dirt underneath.

Opening his eyes, he realized that the brush must have closed right back over him because it was truly dark where he lay. One thing though, he had seemed to have landed in mud or something. It was sticky and he seemed to be laying face down in it. One breath was all it took to tell him the true state of affairs though. One or more of the horses must have been through here, because although it was too dark to see what he was laying in, his nose could not be fooled. He was laying in a large pile of fresh horse manure.

He started to recoil away from it, but just then the younger of the two men spoke from right above him on the bank. "Somethin' was botherin' the horses fer sure. Din't you hear the crash when he took off across the river here?"

From the other, "Wal, it mighta been anythin'. A deer, or a elk. Shoot, you got lions er bear er some other fool thing on yer mind an ya can't seem to get it out."

"Yeah, well, you might remember just last month, they was a bear come down to Silverton, over there. If some bear was to spook our hosses, you'd be the first one a bawlin' as you walked outa here, now that I know."

The other snorted, "You're a long way frum Silverton. An' shoot, they ain' enough bears 'round 'bout here to worry 'bout the way you do."

This seemed to be a rather emotionless argument, carried on more for its entertainment and time passing value between the two, than for any trying to convince the other. Of course they didn't know that Jasper was near to smothering right below them with his face in a pile of horse droppings and the inability to move a muscle for fear of alerting them.

They went on arguing in the same vein until Jasper knew he'd have to do something shortly. He held his breath for as long as he could, then tried to take extremely shallow breaths. It just wasn't enough to sustain him. Finally, he could hold out no longer. He tipped his head up a little and tried to take a quiet deep breath. It didn't come out that way. Involuntarily, his breath whooshed in in a gasping hiss.

He heard the men above take startled steps back. The young one said. "That there's a rattlersnake if I ever hear'd one. Git back. Ya wanta get bit?"

The older of the two seemed to have a slight catch in his breath too as he answered gamely, "Shoot, constipated lions. Bears. An now a rattler. I swear if you ain' the most nervous feller. Ya din' used to be thata way." But his voice was fading as he followed the other at a good pace.

The other must have been nearly running away, because his voice was very faint. But it was still strong enough that Jasper clearly heard, "I'm agonna get my gun and a flashlight. That there rattlersnake is turned up at the wrong place this time."

Jasper was still gasping, trying to make up for the time of mostly no breathing. He knew that he had to leave now though, before the young one got back with his light and gun. He leaped up and ran for the trail. The trouble was that in his haste and fear of the gun that might be on its way, he completely forgot that there was a river between him and the trail. That fact was brought to his attention in the, as usual for him, unpleasant manner. He ran right off a low bank into a pool.

The pool was relatively shallow, coming only to Jaspers waist when he stood. The trouble was that when he fell in, he wasn't standing. He hit the river stretched at full length and went completely under. The icy water took his breath away, seemed to just freeze him solid for a moment. When he could finally move again, he had a moments rational thought as he took in what he'd done and took a second to scrub his beard to try to clean the horse dropping from it. He just couldn't take the time needed to clean it though, and after a cursory few rubs, he splashed out and ran through the brush until he stumbled out on the trail.

He immediately turned and began to run full speed up the trail, but after he began to climb, the thought hit that the trail would be in full view of the meadow for most of the way to the top. It was fairly dark and he really didn't think that the men in the meadow would be able to see that far, but on second thought, he wasn't willing to bet his life on it.

There was a sizable side canyon taking off to the east just at the bottom of the hill he was climbing and without hesitation, he turned and retraced his steps to the bottom and turned up the canyon.

The brush and trees were thick in the canyon bottom and gave him real trouble until after a few hundred feet he stumbled onto a game trail that was well beaten and easy to follow. He was able to take this at a run and he did because he needed the exercise to try to warm himself up as much as to get away from any pursuer. The water of the river had been icy and the breeze he was raising by running made the wet clothes seem to be made of solid ice. The exertion of his headlong pace kept him feeling fairly warm though.

About half a mile along the trail, the canyon steepened quickly and the trail began to switchback up the side of the slope. It went up so steep that after a few of the switchbacks, he had to stop and rest. With the stop though, the tiny breeze cut through the wet clothes and within minutes he was shaking and shivering so hard that his teeth clacked. He decided that he'd have to govern his speed to balance with his strength so he could keep moving and not have to stop. He had no doubt that to stop tonight for any length of time would likely cause some kind of sickness or maybe even worse. He doubted that he'd ever been in a more serious situation.

It took most of an hour to top out the ridge at the slower speed. He stopped and looked down his back trail. There was nothing visible, but he couldn't stop for long at all because of the fairly strong wind up here that took only seconds to cause him to feel as if he was literally freezing. He moved on down the other side of the ridge.

He found that moving down the other side of the ridge on the steep trail fast enough to keep warm was impossible. The exercise wasn't strenuous enough going down and even approaching a speed that might have kept him warm, had him moving so fast that he couldn't control his descent. After a couple of near disasters, he slowed to a safe pace and just shivered.

It was when he neared the bottom that the knowledge of something not quite fitting filtered through. He stopped and looked at a faint flickering glow a couple of hundred yards to the west. He realized that he'd been seeing it for quite some time, but had been too miserable for the significance to filter through.

Now, through his shivering and shaking, he realized that someone had a campfire up the canyon just a short way. The fact that it might have been someone that he definitely wouldn't want to see, seemed irrelevant right then. He moved off the trail into the thick brush toward the glow.

Trying to move through the brush quietly and yet sufficiently quick enough to get there before he froze seemed an impossible compromise. Both things seemed to telescope time so that it was impossible to know how long it took before he was eventually just a thin brush away from a small blazing fire. He could see a few cooking utensils here and there and slung from a slanting stick to hang over the center of the fire, there was a kettle from which steam was spouting.

There didn't seem to be anyone around though. Just to the side, there seemed to be a large rock with some kind of fur robe spread over it. Something shiny reflected the firelight near the top of the pile of fur. This he paid little attention because all he could see was the fire and the warmth it represented. The fur seemed to move just a little and he was startled, even in his desperate condition to hear a voice emanate from it. "Howdy doo neighbor. Don' stan' on cer'mony. Come rat on in an have a seat to the far. It do be a chilly night, now don' it?"

Jasper lost no time at all in moving to the fire and leaning over, tried to encompass all the heat it had. He could never remember anything at all that had felt even close to as good as the heat did. For the next few minutes, he wasn't aware of anything but the fire and its heat. If the other said anything at all, he missed it.

Chapter Six

As the urgency to get next to the fire abated somewhat, Jaspers natural politeness began to resurface. Turning his head to the other to thank him, he hesitated. Thinking about it, he could see no way this could be a joke, but this had all the marks of a setup. The illusion of some kind of fur rug or robe spread over a rock was only reinforced by a pair of thick glasses setting on a blade of nose. The top of the fur was about man height, if a man were sitting down, but except for the glasses and the nose, there was nothing but fur to be seen. "Uh, I do want to thank you. This here fire 'bout near saved my life, I can tell you that."

The pile of fur stirred and then leaned forward. The lenses of the glasses seemed to be disconcertingly aimed a little to the left of Jasper. He decided that he must be seeing it wrong. "Why neighbor, yu justa welcome as the day be long. Feel free ta let yore stick float jus' as yore suited."

This speech didn't seem to make much sense to Jasper, but he lost the thought for a moment as some things about the others appearance cleared up. What he was seeing was indeed mostly fur. Some kind of shaggy fur coat that covered the other entirely, His feet must have been curled under him because nothing of them was visible. It must have fit close around his neck, but now it was clear that the other had an impressive beard spreading down to midchest. It was much the same color as the fur coat and the two were indistinguishable in the dim firelight. He had his arms folded over his middle and his hands must have been inside the sleeves. The crowning touch was a shaggy head of hair and facial whiskers that were more widespread than any Jasper had ever seen.

Looking the other closely in the face, he confirmed that there was absolutely nothing of his skin visible except for the nose. His hair completely covered his forehead to his glasses and they reflected the firelight so that nothing at all could be seen of his eyes. He could make no guess at all as to the others age. There was no gray showing in the hair or beard at all but he knew that some people didn't get gray hair until late in life. For some reason, he had an idea that the man was around fifty or sixty. It was just a feeling though and he realized that it had no basis.

Shutting his own eyes for a moment and shaking his head slightly to clear it, Jasper said "Excuse me, I guess I must of heard you wrong. Did you say something about a stick floatin'?" Then remembering his manners, "My name is Jasper Cain."

"Ah'm plumb pleased to meet ya, neighbor Jasper. Jim Bridger be mah handle. As fer the stick afloatin', din' ya nevah read no stories 'bout mountin men. They is all the time asayin' thangs 'bout how they stick be afloatin' an how thangs shine an how they be plumb froze fer beaver an' meat an' one thang 'nother. Jus'a way a talkin', is all it be."

Jasper may have been a little deficient in mountain man folklore, but he had read of Jim Bridger and thought that the coincidence of the name might be a little much. "I see. sticks floatin means kinda the way things happen, is that it? Jim Bridger. seems I heard a that name somewhere."

The top pile of fur with the glasses nodded comfortably. "Sho' you have. Mah name, leastways the one ah wuz born wif, is Homer Funtzt." He snorted, "Now ah ast ya, whut kinda name fer a mountain man be Homer Funtzt? Nah, when ah decided to come up heah to ta mountins and be a mountin man, ah figgered ah hadda git a mountain man name. Ain' hardly no more mountain man name than Jim Bridger, would ya say?"

This seemed like such a novel idea to Jasper that he just stared at the other for a moment, forgetting to answer. Catching himself, he quickly made amends. "I do agree with you. Jim Bridger is a fine mountain man name." He was feeling much warmer, but the conversation along with the smell that still strongly emanated from his beard had him feeling like Alice in Wonderland.

Suddenly the smell from his beard was more than he could stand. "Say Jim...Is it ok to call you Jim?" He took a quaking of the top fur for assent. "Yeah Jim. I got to wash up some. Is there a stream close by somewhere?"

"Why sho' an' they be. Rat behint ya a ways, they be a leetle stream. Cold though, it be."

"Cold or not, I gotta wash up. Thanks." He made his way directly back for several feet before hearing water running off to his right. He found the stream there without any more trouble, but before he stooped to wash, he paused to wonder why Jim had sent him in the wrong direction. He supposed that he'd just misunderstood him. Shrugging he stooped to wash.

One thing that Jim was sure enough right about was that the water was cold. Cold didn't really get it. This was liquid ice. He wondered how water that cold could stay liquid instead of freezing solid. He scrubbed his beard with a little sand from the stream bottom and he felt that it did some good for the smell. But as he got up and took a deep breath, he still smelled the horse manure. He stood and regarded the stream, considering more washing, but he was shivering again. His clothes hadn't got dry and he'd got a little wetter as he washed. In the end he hurried back to the fire.

He'd no more than embraced the heat again than Jim allowed. "Am'm plumb froze fer thet stew rat there, friend Jasper. If'n you wuz to git us a couple a bowls outa that there pack," he gestured to a pack propped against a tree to the side. "Why we kin git us somepin in our bellies. How do that sound?"

Jasper hadn't been aware of hunger, probably because of all the other things that had plagued him this livelong day. Now, even as he heard about the stew, the hunger came roaring like a lion.

He quickly dug out a couple of bowls and spoons from the pack. As he turned back to the fire, he discovered Jim standing. He saw that Jim really did have legs and feet. The coat came only to midcalf length, revealing well worn boots that were so scuffed as to defy analysis of their origin. The rest of him looked the same though, except higher in the air.

Jim didn't seem to see the bowl and spoon that Jasper thrust at him. Finally, he peered down and accepted it. Jasper thought that Jim might be having trouble seeing in the dim light. Jim scooped out a bowl of stew and settled back to his seat, his feet again disappearing under the bottom of the coat. For a second, Jasper wondered if he'd imagined them.

Jim waved to the pot, "Neighbor Jasper, jus' mek yuse'f ta home. Git yo se'f some a thet stew now, ah kin see yore plum' froze fer nourishment."

Jasper lost no time in complying with the invitation. His bowl full, he settled back and dug in. The stew was hot and felt good going down, but there was definitely something about this stuff. Jasper frowned. He put the bowl to his nose and sniffed. He wrinkled his nose at the horse dropping smell that lingered in spite of twice being washed. It must be just the horse smell that was distorting his olfactory organs.

He took another bite. This time, he was sure that there was something about the stew. A subtle flavor that was becoming less subtle with time. He stared down into the bowl. He didn't want to insult Jim, but he had to ask. "Uh...say there Jim. Mighty fine stew here, but I was justa wonderin', what kinda stew you suppose this is?"

Without looking up from his eating chores, Jim answered, "Why neighbor Jasper, this heah be beaver stew."

Jasper looked down into the bowl. He wasn't sure how he felt about beaver stew. After thinking about it a short while, he guessed that it was all right. After all beavers didn't eat anything but wood and they swim in water all the time. They ought to be clean. He took another bite. It seemed that the taste was stronger, but he didn't want to say anything else about it.

Jim solved his dilemma by declaring, "Ah were down ta the stream thar this aftahnoon." He'd again indicated a direction that wasn't the way to the stream. Jasper decided that it had to be the dim light that had Jim confused. "Ah'se on muh way back, plumb froze fer some heat an fire, when this yere beaver come a walkin' along rat in front a me an' jus' as big as yu please. Wal now, ah ast yu, din't ol mister beaver end up in the stew now?"

Jasper had a feeling that if he could have seen Jims face, there would have been a large smirk there. Jasper had, by this time, eaten most of the bowl of stew. The taste continued to bother him, being strong enough to come through even the horse dropping smell by now.

Jim waved a negligent hand at a bush to the side. "Ah skint 'im out an' put 'im in the stew. Looka there at his pelt. Fan pelt, don' it be?"

Jasper looked that way vaguely. Something about the pelt hanging on the bush didn't look just right. The bush was off a few feet and the light very dim there, but he could swear that he could see some white on it. "Say Jim, what color is a beaver? I always thought they was brown."

"Why, an brown is whut they be. Why fer yu askin' 'bout 'em, friend Jasper?"

"Well, that there one............." Jasper was truly puzzled now. He'd looked closer and could definitely see some white. He sat his bowl on a nearby rock and rising, walked over to the pelt. He didn't need to go close. He didn't even really have to look. As he got near, the smell cut through the other smells to confirm that he was indeed looking at a skunk. "Uh Jim. This here.. uh..beaver. Is he the one you made that there stew from?"

Jim was still unconcernedly eating and paid no attention other than a cursory glance. "Thet be him rat thar on thet thar bush. Thet pelt shines, now don' it?"

Jasper stood wondering. How could Jim have killed and skinned the skunk without knowing that it was a skunk. Jim seemed incapable of joking about it. The only thing Jasper could think of was maybe he couldn't see very well. The thought had no more came than it grew. The thick glasses. Not seeming to know where the stream was. "When did you get him Jim?"

"It were jus' comin' onto dark, neighbor Jasper. Got 'im good though."

Walking back and setting down, Jasper considered. "Uh..da you smell anything strange Jim?"

The top fur swung this way and that as Jim presumably tested the air for smells. "Why no, friend Jasper. ah don' smell nothin." The mountain of fur rolled forward a bit as Jim presumably moved into confiding range. "Ah will say though, jus' to yu neighbor Jasper, thet ever since ah had some kinda fever sev'ral yars back, my sniffer ain' been whut it once were. Whut wuz it that yu thank yu wuz a smellin'?" he finished politely.

Jaspers mouth had fallen open at the confidence. That was the answer to the why of the skunk stew. Jim hadn't been able to smell it. That still left the riddle of how he hadn't been able to see the black and white of the pelt, but Jasper was willing to grant that he might not be able to see good in the dim light. Now he tardily answered, "Ah...why it was nothin' Jim. I jus' thought I mighta smelled a skunk, was all."

Jim nodded dismissively "Have yuse'f some mo' a thet stew, neighbor Jasper. Ah do b'lieve ah'll have a bit more a it mase'f." Jim rose and moved ponderously forward to take more stew in his bowl.

"Ah..no thanks Jim. I've had a plenty." He rose and as Jim moved back to his seat and began to eat, Jasper moved back to embrace the fire. He wondered if he'd ever be entirely warm again. The night air was definitely becoming frosty and although he was able to get warm on the side that was to the fire, the side away from it would begin to shiver. He got so close to the fire that he began to steam before turning the cold side to do the same. His clothes were beginning to dry but it was going to get a lot colder before it got warmer tomorrow. "Ah Jim, you think it might be alright if I was to stay by yore fire tonight? These clothes haven't dried very good an' it's gettin' kinda cold."

Jims glasses swung his way again. And again, Jasper thought that Jim settled his glance on a spot somewhere off to his side. "Wet clothes, do ya say, neighbor Jasper. Whut air yu adoin' wif wet clothes? Kinda late fer clothes washin', wouldn' ya say?" A strangled sounding "Heh, heh, heh" emanated from the mountain of fur and seismic waves seemed to ripple up and down.

Jasper managed a weak "Ha ha. Ah no, it was this way, I kinda fell in the river." He hadn't imagined that Jim wouldn't have noticed that his clothes were wet. "I sure would appreciate it though, if I could share yore fire tonight."

"Why yu bet, friend Jasper. Ah wuz justa gonna ast ya enyhow. Won' hurt to leave yo' own camp fer the night?"

"Uh..well, my camps quite a ways off. It's a kind of a long story. It seems like I'm so sleepy that I can't think good. If it's ok, I'll just hunker down here and try to get some sleep." He wasn't telling any lie either. As he'd got warmer, the whole day had seemed to catch up with him suddenly and he found he could hardly keep his eyes open.

Jim nodded equably. "Jus take that thar blanket under the pack, neighbor Jasper. Ah c'n make out wif muh coat. Stretch rat out thar wharever place shines to yu."

Jasper nodded gratefully as he quickly moved to get the blanket and snuggle down into it. With the welcome warmth, he seemed to drop immediately into a bottomless pit.

Chapter Seven

Jasper came awake suddenly with a sense of startled strangeness. He lay for a moment trying to remember where he was before cracking an eyelid slightly. He was facing some trees and bushes and they seemed far different than the ones he was used to. Trees and bushes being much the same most places up in the mountains though, he paid that little attention. He thought it must have been something else that had disturbed him.

There was a slight clink of metal hitting metal behind him that caused him to leap to a sitting position and whirl to look behind defensively.

There was a large bear standing just the other side of a roaring fire. He was half way to his feet in a spontaneous and unconscious leap when memory flooded in. Jim regarded him curiously, again seeming to look past his shoulder.

The sun was just coming over the eastern ridges and the light was good. He certainly could be forgiven for mistaking Jim for a bear, he thought. Except for the thick glasses, the resemblance was impressive. The coat had long fur of some kind and even in this better light, it was difficult to see where the coat began and the beard ended. Standing and facing Jasper, the other was little more than a mountain of fur. While only a little taller than Jasper, he had broad shoulders and an impressive girth around the middle. "Mo'nin friend Jasper. Heh, heh, heh. Did ah skeer ya jus' a bit? Heh, heh, heh."

Jaspers heart was still beating erratically and it took a conscious effort to replay with a weak, "Ha, ha. Well, just a little Jim. Guess I wasa sleeping deep, still."

"Wal, jus set up here, neighbor Jasper. Ah got us some fried beaver fer breakfust." Jim handed him a plate.

Jasper stared down on a haunch of some kind of small animal. The first thing he'd smelled this morning was the residue of the horse manure. He wondered how long it would take to wear off entirely. Now he bent his head to the plate and sniffed. Could he smell skunk? "Uh...say Jim, this wouldn't be some a that beaver that you made stew from, now would it?"

"Wal, an' it wud be, friend Jasper. Shoot, ah din' need him all fer thet thar stew. Saved plenty fer this yere breakfast. It sho' do shine fer this early mo'nin', now don' it."

Jasper stared at him for a moment before giving up entirely. When he took care not to think about it, the skunk tasted something like chicken. Or at least no worse than a gamey rabbit. As he sat eating and considering his troubles, he forgot what he was eating anyway.

Jim was sitting across the fire unconcernedly eating and as Jasper looked at him, he just had to ask what he was doing here. "Jim, I don't like bein' nosy, but if you wouldn't mind, what are you up here for?"

"Why friend Jasper, ah don min' a bit. Fac a ta mattah, ah'm proud you ast. Leetle a nothin' ta tell though. Ah jus' got sick and tired a them comminists out thar a tellin' me whut ah could an' couldn' do with muh own propity. Ah figger to heck wif 'em. Come up here and don' have to fight 'wif em no more." His voice took on an earnest tone although it was impossible to evaluate his expression under all the cover of beard. "Up heah, ah can be free as a bud er a deer. Ah traps a leetle, prospects a bit. Ah keep outa the way a all those comminists down there. Thas all."

"Is trapping and all that legal?"

"Ah 'spect it ain'. But ah been mostly able ta keep outa they way, and when ah cain', ah jus lies to em. Ain bothered me much so fer."

Jasper took care to hide the amusement he felt, not wanting to take a chance on hurting Jims feelings.

"Say thar, friend Jasper, if'n it wouldn't be ferwerd, ah'd return the favor an' ast 'bout why you be up heah yu own se'f?"

Jasper took a moment to regard the other soberly as he considered. In the end, he told it all just the way it happened, except for editing out the part about acquiring Genevieve. He did however tell of the strong attachment he'd developed for the horse. He wasn't sure that Jim wouldn't hold it against him for the way he'd gone about getting her. He said, by way of explanation of why he was afraid to openly go in and claim her from the rangers, that he'd been trapping and he was afraid that the rangers would find out and impound Genevieve. Like a lot of things lately, he knew this was weak, but Jim didn't seem to notice. He figured that he'd probably see the last of him in a short while anyway. As soon as he could figure what to do about trailing the rangers further, he'd be leaving.

Jims head had tipped forward during the story and he'd been so motionless that Jasper wondered if he'd gone to sleep. As he finished the story, he lapsed into his own silence, thinking of what he should do.

So deep into his deliberations was he that when Jim moved and cleared his throat, Jasper was startled and jumped.

"Friend Jasper, ah'm gone hep yu to git yo' hoss back. Why, ah figger it ain' no more'n muh bound n' duty." The top fur nodded up and down. "Yas suh, we git her back fer yu, yu bet."

Jasper fought to control his sense of incredulity. He wouldn't have hurt Jims feelings for the world but the first thing that came to his mind was the picture of the mountain of fur coming into sight of the rangers. It seemed to him as he thought of it that simply the sight of Jim would excite the suspicions of every authority in the state of Colorado. "Uh..Jim, did ya say that you'd talked to the rangers, er maybe game wardens, whoever?" It was hard to know how to phrase what he wanted to ask. Finally, he came up with, "How do they feel about you wearin that fur coat? Do they think you trapped it?" Jasper thought that was kind of a weak question, but he could come up with nothing better at the moment.

"This yere's a ol' buff'ler coat. Bought it legal long fore ah decided to come up heah. Yeah they knows ah'm up yere alrat. Ah jus' traps and hunts 'nough fer muh needs. Shoot, them there ol' boys is fer too lazy to come achasin' me long's ah keep off the beaten trails. Ta times as ah see 'em, why they all treat me as if ah was ta real Jim Bridger. Yeh friend Jasper, ah c'n be a big he'p ta ya."

Jasper considered. If it was true that the rangers didn't hassle Jim when they saw him, it must be that they considered him kind of crazy. Harmlessly crazy, He supposed. The more he considered it, the more attractive the prospect of company was. Why not?

"Well Jim, if you was to wanta do that, why I can say that I'd welcome the company. Let's do some planning of what and how."

After thirty minutes of going over the available information, the best they could come up with was going back to the meadow and if the rangers were camped there, to try to come up with a plan that would fit the situation.

As they began to get ready to go, something occurred to Jasper. If they were forced to stay on the trail for a period of days, he was going to need more than Jim had available here. If they ended up at the end of the day somewhere too close to the rangers to build a fire, Jim would need his blanket.

"Jim, I'm going to have to go back to my camp to get some things we'll need. I need my sleepin' bag for one thing. An' some other things too, if we was to be on the trail for a long time."

"Wal, neighbor Jasper, jus's yu please. Cain't we pick it up 'long the way?"

"Naw. My camps the other direction. A long way in the other direction. If I start now, I think I can make it there and back by dark. Why don't you get your own things ready to go and if I do get back tonight, why we can go tomorrow first thing. If I don't get back tonight, I still should be here to go in the morning sometime. Thing is, I'm not exactly sure how far I am from my camp. I'll have to go over 'til I cut the trail and then follow it along." As he'd spoken, Jasper realized that he faced a long hard trip of uncertain distance. He'd be going further than he'd done when he trailed the rangers yesterday, because he wasn't about to try going straight over the mountains again. He'd found out the hard way that was too tough.

"Wal, friend Jasper, don' yu worry 'bout one leetle thang. Since ah got some time, why what ah'll do is go on over an' scout the sit'chasen out. Time yu git back, ah orta know jus' whut we need ta do."

Instead of reassuring Jasper, this information mightily alarmed him. "Uh...Jim, you really think ya oughta do that. If them there rangers git a look at ya, they might suspicion som'thin' 'bout what we doin'."

Jim waved a deprecating hand. "Ease yo' mind, neighbor Jasper. Why, whut yu don' re'lize is thet yu lookin' at a real mountin man. Them there boys won' even know ah'm aroun'. Ah'll jus' injun on in there an' have muh look an' then we gone know whuts whut."

Jasper looked at the sun. He had to get going if he had any chance at all of making his camp and getting back today. But Jims last assurance had done anything but reassure him. There was little he could do though if Jim was determined to go scout things out. It could even be a big help if he was really able to get in and look around without the rangers being any the wiser. He did take the time to add this caution. "Jim, if you was to get seen and have to talk to 'em, don' mention nothin' 'bout what we'r doin'."

"Don' trouble yo mind, friend Jasper. Yo secret is as safe..." Jasper didn't hear the rest because he'd already left the campsite and was heading toward the trail.

The trail was about a mile and a half down the canyon. He carefully checked it when he got there for any sign that the rangers had returned along it. Reassuringly, his own tracks were the last that had been here. He turned down toward his camp.

He felt many of yesterdays aches and pains at first but they quickly worked themselves out. It was a good thing that they did because the day proved to be brutal. By resting not at all and keeping his walk to top speed, he made his camp by not much after noon. Try as he might though, he estimated that he was still ten miles short of Jims camp when the sun set that evening. The darkness and complete exhaustion arrived at about the same time. He couldn't go on without rest and he knew it. It was all he could do to struggle off the trail into a nest of thick grass. He shrugged the pack off and used it for a pillow. Thirty seconds after he lay down, he was deep asleep.

Because he hadn't bothered to get in his sleeping bag, he simply hadn't thought of it in his exhaustion, he woke shivering in the formless gray dawn. Five minutes on the trail loosened his muscles and worked up enough heat that he forgot the cold though.

The sun had been up an hour when he got to Jims' camp. Jim was up and had something frying on the fire. "Wal, friend Jasper. Yu a lookin' pert this yere mo'nin'. Sit up ta the far an' have some a this yere beaver."

"Beaver? I thought yu cooked the last a that yesterday."

"Wal, an' ah did. Ah did neighbor Jasper. This yere is 'nother one."

Jasper had had all the skunk he intended to eat. "Where you say that there pelt is. Of this here last one you got, I mean?"

"Why, it be rat thar by t'other one, friend Jasper."

Shucking his pack off, Jasper moved over and regarded the pelt. This one was clearly no skunk. It was just as clearly no beaver either. It had long ears and a fluffy tail. As he regarded the rabbit skin, it occurred to him just how hungry he was. He'd managed to gather a few roots yesterday when he'd passed close to a marsh, but had had nothing else.

He moved back to the fire and got his tin plate from his pack. "I believe I will have some a that beaver, Jim. It do smell fine."

While Jasper ate, Jim told of his adventures yesterday. They could best be described as anticlimactic. The meadow had been empty and there had been no sign of horses or men to be seen. "Don' worry none though, friend Jasper. Ah gotta line on 'em. Ah know jus' whar they be headed. Soon's yo' ready, we cut acrost ta ridge heah an' pick up they tracks. Foller 'em rat along, yu bet."

"The ridge right here, you mean? The trail goes along the other canyon bottom. You sure you mean right over here Jim?"

"Yasser. Ah picked they tracks up agoin' rat thisaway over the ridge thar. Foller 'em on the run, 'bout near, when yu git ready."

Jasper was about ready and he checked to see what Jim was taking. Jim had packed a light pack consisting of little more than his blanket. He packed his rifle now, which was the first that Jasper had seen of it. He hadn't known that Jim had one. It was an ancient cap and ball long rifle. Jasper asked to look at it, and when it was handed to him, he sincerely praised it. He'd seen them before but had never actually held one. He hated to hand it back and resolved to ask to shoot it when this was over. Now Jim stood and took off his coat. He said he'd leave it as it wasn't conducive to fast traveling. Jasper took a moment to look at what he wore under the coat. It was a complete buckskin suit, even to the rawhide fringes on every seam. Jim was big and it showed now the coat was off. He was fat, but it seemed that the fat was over muscle. He moved lightly and easily.

It took Jasper only moments to empty his pack of most of the nonessentials in it. He took little more than Jim had, just his sleeping bag, his small canteen and some cooking utensils.

Thirty minutes after they'd started, they were over the ridge and had come to the trail. "Wal, friend Jasper, rat thar they be." He pointed to a trail through the brush that had been torn up and beaten down by many animals passage. Jasper moved up to look.

Something didn't seem just right to him. "Jim, these tracks ain't horse tracks."

Jim regarded him solemnly. "Neighbor Jasper, it be a good thang thet yu got me to steer ya on. Ah know yu ain' famil'ar with how these yere redskins fool ya. They alas use buff'ler tracks to hide they own. Why, it be the kinda thin' they alas do." He nodded his head affirmatively.

"But Jim, these rangers wasn't no redskins. They was jus' folks. An' these here ain' buffalo tracks either." But it suddenly occurred to him that he'd never seen a buffalo track, so how could he be sure. He plowed ahead anyway. "I jus' don' see no horse tracks there."

Jim gave him an archly superior look. He bent to the trail and pointed. "Now yu justa lookee here, friend Jasper, an' ah'll edi'cate ya a bit. Whut is it that ya see?"

Jasper went to one knee to get close and see what Jim was trying to show him. This particular part of the trail was so torn up that he couldn't even discern any elk or deer tracks, just scuffed ground. He looked at Jim, "What is it that you see? I can't see nothin'."

Jim regarded him with astonishment. "Why friend Jasper, it be as plain as the nose on yo face. Lookee rat heah, don' that be a hoss track?" He pointed to one of the most torn up sections of the torn up section. "It do be." He answered his own question triumphantly.

Again Jasper bent his gaze to the ground. This time he got so close that he rammed his nose into the dust a little and it made him sneeze. There was something there. He supposed there was a possibility that it might be a horse track. After all, Jim had had a lot more experience with tracks than him. "You sure that there's a horse track, are ya Jim?"

"Why, airy a us mountain mens takes pride in bein' able to track on ta run, friend Jasper. Jus' set yo' mind ta ease an' foller along. They got 'bout near a days lead, but we'll come up to 'em. Never fear."

Jim moved out along the trail, following it up the canyon. Jasper still had qualms about the whole thing. He stood a moment looking back the way the trail came, but Jim was moving right along and after just a short hesitation, Jasper hurried after him.

The tracks followed the canyon bottom for a couple of miles until the bottom began to rise in a series of small cliffs. Just before they got there, the trail led off across the creek and up the south slope at a steep transverse angle. The climb took an hour and winded them both to the point that they had to take a long rest at the top.

From there, the tracks took off across lush meadows where wildflowers were beginning to bloom in the spring sunshine.

They stopped briefly at noon and ate the remainder of the `beaver'. Shortly after they started trailing again, the tracks dipped into a deep canyon. It led them around cliffs and impenetrable thickets of scrub oak until they reached the bottom. Whenthey finally got there, it was a beautiful place. Nearly a half mile wide and with thick green grass and pine trees widely spaced. Jasper found himself hoping that the rangers had stopped someplace down here, but no such luck.

The tracks led straight across and Jim and Jasper followed straight across. They did however, stop at the crystal clear creek that flowed through the bottom to get a drink and take a breather. It was while they were there that Jim made a little brag. "Din' ah tell yu, friend Jasper, thet ah could trail these yere tracks on ta run?"

"You did, Jim. You surely did." Jasper didn't tell him what he really felt, which was that so far, even he could have trailed the tracks at a run, they were so prominently beaten into what was mostly smooth untouched ground. He didn't say it because he did really appreciate Jims efforts and company. He was glad Jim was along.

The tracks led straight across and up the far slope. By the time they topped out that ridge, the sun had gone behind the western hills. Both were so tired that they elected to simply roll into their bedrolls without the benefit of a fire. They had nothing to cook anyway.

As tired as they were, the night seemed to pass almost instantly. It was to a chilly breakfastless sunup that they awoke. After laying there thinking about it, Jasper decided that they'd better find something to eat or they'd be played out long before they were ever able to catch the rangers.

He had a drink of water, which seemed to do little to fill him. While Jim was up fussing around and loosening his muscles, Jasper walked back to the edge of the canyon. There was a rock slide just below the rim and just as he got to the edge, he noticed movement down the slide aways. He stood still and after a moment was rewarded with the sight of a large rockchuck moving onto a rock to sun himself.

Moving as quietly and carefully as possible, Jasper got back out of line of sight before whirling and running back to the campsite. "Jim, there's a 'chuck sunnin' hisself over there on the slide. Git yore gun an le's get some breakfast." Jasper had left his twenty two back at the camp, thinking he'd have no use for it.

Jim grabbed his rifle and hissed, "Le's git 'im. Ah sho am hongry."

"Well, come on. Let's crawl over to the edge an' I'll show 'im to ya." Jasper moved over to the canyon edge. He could hear Jim following and paid him no more attention until he got to the edge and laid down. "Ya see 'im right there, Jim?" He asked in a low whisper.

"Whar at, is 'e? Ah cain' see 'im." Jim asked back in a low hissing voice.

"Well, see him right there on that rock. Big ol' rockchuck right there. Shoot 'im."

"Oh. Rat. Ah see 'im now 'e's moved."

Jasper had been looking right at the chuck and he hadn't seen any move, but as long as Jim could see him, that was alright.

The thumping blast of the rifle took him by surprise. He hadn't even seen Jim aim, and he'd thought he would since Jim would have to put the rifle down past his head to shoot. His heart dropped as he saw the rockchuck jump up and still alive and lively, disappear into his hole under the rock. He could feel the empty in his stomach get even emptier.

Jim jumped up and hollered, "Ah got 'im. Build up the far, friend Jasper."

Jasper turned to head to inform Jim that he hadn't got anything, only to see him loping toward a tree at the canyon rim about twenty feet away. He quickly climbed to his feet to follow. Jim was standing over something in the grass and as Jasper came up, he turned and regarded him sadly. "Friend Jasper, ah do b'lieve ah'm ashamed a yu."

Jasper, confused and still not having seen what Jim had shot, frowned and asked, "What is it that you mean, Jim?"

"Wal, this here ain' no rock chuck, now be it?"

It was at this point that Jasper saw what Jim had shot. It was a wild turkey. "But, the chuck was over there." He said defensively as he pointed down to the slide.

Jim sighed. "Don' make it no mo' shameful than it be, friend Jasper. Ah'll teach yu 'bout things, but we is gotta be careful 'bout what it be we shoot up yere."

Jasper couldn't figure what the other was talking about. To his way of thinking, it would have been hard to get anything better than the turkey to eat. Much better than the rockchuck he thought. "Well Jim, this here will make mighty good eatin', Don' ya think?"

Jim shook his head sadly. "Wal, ah guess we might's well eat 'im, but ah gotta tell ya, friend Jasper, ah don' like the idee a shooting, an' then eatin' this yere eagle."

Chapter Eight

The turkey had been quite large, dressing out at probably around ten pounds. There wasn't a whole lot left when they were done and ready to take the trail again. They'd put it over the fire on a spit, but didn't feel that they could take the time to cook it properly because of their hurry to get on the tracks. Both were hungry enough that they didn't want to wait on that account either. It ended up with the outside burned nearly black and the inside still nearly raw, but nothing had tasted quite that good for a long time to either of them.

Jim had spent a good part of the meal grumbling about how he felt bad about eating an eagle the way he was. Jasper wouldn't have hurt his feelings for the world, but he wondered how it was that Jim could possibly have mistaken the turkey for an eagle. Allowing for a superficial color similarity, the turkey had the usual red head and wattles under the chin that no self respecting eagle would have ever stood for.

He kept quiet about the whole thing though and when they were ready to go, Jim had seemed to forget the episode in his enthusiasm for following the tracks.

For most of the morning, the tracks seemed content to follow along the top of the mountain chain. Most of it was fairly level meadow land with rolling undulations that were infinitely easier going than that of yesterday.

About noon, the trail led down into a small canyon, which it crossed and climbed the other side. When they got to the top, they could see more open meadow through about a quarter mile of scattered bushes. The tracks led straight to it.

As they approached the clearing edge, Jim slowed down and held his hand up for Jasper to stop. "Lemme injun on up thar an' see if'n them thar ol' boys is out thar, neighbor Jasper."

Jasper was glad to comply. He was tired out from the crossing down into and out of the last canyon. Jim moved quietly up to the clearing edge and paused there motionless. He did that for so long that Jasper finally moved after him. "What d'ya see, Jim?"

They were behind a thin bush that Jasper thought would hide them adequately if they remained still. Jim turned and put a warning hand on his shoulder. "They be out thar, friend Jasper. See 'em rat 'crost thar. Ain' been doin' nothin' but standin', leastways mostly."

Jasper looked. The bush restricted his sight and although it was clear that something was over there alright, nearly a quarter of a mile away, something just didn't seem right about it. He tried to raise up to get a better view, but Jim pushed him down with a warning "Shhhhh." Looking down, he thought that he might be able to see under the bush. Jim seemed to have no objection to his dropping to the ground and he found that there was indeed a clear space there. He could see clearly with no impediment of branches whatever.

It was just possible that he could see too clearly. Across the clearing and close to the far side grazed eight large elk. Was this what Jim had been looking at? He craned his neck this way and that. The clearing was roughly circular and he could see virtually all of it from his vantage point. There was absolutely nothing there with the exception of the small herd of elk.

"Dog--gone it Jim. There ain' nothin'..." he caught himself. He was whispering and there was no reason now for doing so. "Dog--gone it Jim, there ain a thing out there 'cepting some elk." He said in a somewhat louder than normal voice.

"Shhh..." Shushed Jim before catching what Jasper had said. "Elks?" He asked as he gave a frown. He raised his head over the bush top to get a clear look. "Elks? Yu mean whut ah been a seein' yere is elks?" He shook his head sadly as he thought about it. "Wal, Mus' be thet them thar fellers turned off some'ers. acourse, we is b'hint 'em a ways. Them thar elks musta come on ta paster thar since them thar fellers lef'."

For a moment, Jaspers hopes soared, but he knew as he thought about it, just how unlikely it was. He'd thought from the first that they were trailing elk. He'd never seen a horse track on the trail that he himself could clearly identify. He'd finally just quit looking at it and took Jim at his word that they were there. While he knew that they'd have go out and check the tracks to see for sure what had happened, right now he just wanted to rest for awhile.

He'd carried the remains of the turkey along, although there had been little left after they both got enough this morning. Now he looked around for a grassy spot to sit down and have some of it. For some reason, going out into the meadow didn't appeal to him. For one thing, he really didn't want to spook the elk off their feed ground since they'd got there first. He spotted a small clearing off to the side and close to some thick brush. He moved that way.

He got out the turkey and set it on his pack before turning and hollering just loud enough for Jim to hear, "Come on Jim. We'll have the rest a this turkey 'fore we go on."

Jim was still staring out at the clearing and from time to time Jasper could hear some low grumbling. Now he turned and beckoned Jasper back. When he got close, Jim whispered, "Friend Jasper, ah thank them thar fellers must be a layin' up out thar somers. Why, we know they been a usin' them elks fer to hide they tracks. Ah do b'lieve they is alayin' up rat out thar in the middle. Take a look an' see. Rat in the middle, ah c'n see 'em."

Nothing could have galvanized Jasper into faster action, improbable though the concept of the rangers laying up in the center of the meadow was. He again took his vantage point of before, under the bush. There was an old log out toward the middle but other than that, there was just nothing. "You mean that log out there, Jim?"

Jim had never quit staring out there, and he continued for a few moments more before answering, "Thet thar log be a hidey fer 'em, ah'm a thinkin'."

Jasper looked again before he questioned, "Well what would they be doin' hidin' Jim. They don't know we're a follerin', now do they?"

Jim looked at him in surprise. "Wal..Ah...They mighta...." He stuttered. He'd evidently never bothered to think of a reason for them hiding out there and he acted as though being forced to contemplate such practical matters was not to his liking.

"Well look Jim. What say we get over there an' finish off that turkey. We can check that trail out, after."

Jim bent an inquisitive look on him. "Whut turkey would thet be, neighbor Jasper?"

"Uh...What I meant was that eagle. Yeah, we can finish up the eagle."

"Wal, alrat. After, why we c'n git rat 'long after them thar fellers agin. Ah tell yu neighbor Jasper, we ain' fer behint 'em now. Ah jus' got a feelin'." He moved off towards where Jasper had set the turkey out.

Jasper remained for a moment, staring out at the log and wondering if Jim could be right. There was nothing out by it moving at all though and he finally stood up and turned to follow. He'd no more than turned when Jim burst through the brush where Jasper had left the turkey. He screeched, "Run. Oh, run fer yo laf, friend Jasper."

His urgency was such that Jasper turned and ran even as he questioned over his shoulder, "What?" He was up to full speed before he again questioned Jim with a bellered, "What?" If Jim answered, he didn't hear him, but that might have been because it was at that moment that he picked to stumble over a thickly laced bush. His legs tangled and he pitched forward into another bush. It served to break his fall so he at least didn't slam into the ground very hard.

Just as he pushed himself up on his arms, Jim, either because he didn't see him, or maybe he just needed some good way to get over the bushes, stomped right in the middle of his back. Jims weight smashed him deeper into the bush and further into the ground than he'd went before.

He picked his head up and spit a mouthful of brush and dirt out as he saw Jim leap and grab a limb on a fair sized tree and go up like a squirrel. That's all he had time to see before something even heavier than Jim used him for the same purpose; to get over the bushes.

This time, he was smashed into the ground so hard that in spite of the remains of the bush under him acting as a weak shock absorber, his breath was partially knocked away. He picked his head up and looked for what it was that had committed this last hit and run. His eyes got big as he saw a large black bear reach the tree that Jim was still climbing. The bear didn't even hesitate. It started up the tree as easily as if it were walking on level ground. Jim looked down at the climbing bear and gave a great squall.

Jasper didn't understand the content of what Jim had said and right then he didn't care. He'd been ill used to the point that it didn't matter right at that moment, who got who up that tree.

He jumped up and with what breath he could gather, screamed, "Dog--gone it." This didn't let off quite enough steam and he grabbed his cap off to throw it down and stomp it. Just then though, he noticed that the bear had stopped climbing and was looking back at him. He belatedly knew that the scream had attracted its attention. He carefully returned his cap to his head and began to slowly back off.

The bear obviously wasn't stupid. He saw something right on the ground that would be far easier to get than what he was climbing this tree for. It let go and hit the ground running.

"Eeeeeeee...." Jasper screamed as he turned and charged away. The area toward the clearing was more clear of brush than any other direction and Jasper took the route of least resistance.

As he burst through the brush at the clearing edge, he came face to face with several large animals. It took a split second to see that they were the elk who had become curious about all the noise and had come to investigate. The split second was too much though. He'd already tried to come to a panic stop and that had tangled his legs. He slammed forward to the ground yet again. As he was falling, he saw that the elk had been equally startled and had swapped ends and bolted with loud snorts.

He'd no more than raised his face from the dirt again than the bear yet again used him for a floor mat. This time there was no bush to soften the weight that bore him down and his body and face was shoved deep into the dirt and mud.

He raised bleary eyes to see the bear chasing the elk at full speed. He realized that by falling, he'd disappeared from the bears view at the same time that the larger and more attractive elk had appeared in it. The bear, being a sensible animal had decided that the elk were a much more desirable target. It clearly had only run over Jasper by chance. His last look that way revealed that the elk were gaining on the still pursuing bear. They all disappeared into the tree line on the far side of the clearing.

He decided that it was lucky that there'd been mud to fall in. It had provided a soft place for his face to go. It was only then that he noticed that where his head had come down was the only soft muddy place around. At about the same time, he noticed that something didn't smell just right. He looked down. What he had shoved his face in wasn't mud, it was a large pile of fresh elk droppings. In spite of still being short of breath he jumped up and screamed, "Dog--gone it." That not being enough, he completed the aborted gesture of a minute ago, tearing off his cap and jumping up and down on it while he continued his abusive tirade of, "Dog--gones."

Jim picked that moment to walk up and inform him, "Friend Jasper. It do appear thet yu got somepin smeared all 'round 'bout in yo' beard."

Chapter Nine

It might have been one of the toughest things Jasper had ever done, but he got his temper under control before saying anything to Jim that he'd have later regretted. The effort took a minute, but Jim wasn't watching or aware of it anyway. He'd walked past Jasper and was looking at the tracks there. Turning to Jasper, he observed, "Neighbor Jasper, yu reckon thet them thar fellers we wuz a follerin' along mighta got scared off by that thar bar?"

Jasper had already counted to ten and he was able now, with an effort, to answer in a civil manner. "I don' know Jim." He took a moment more before he said, "What say we have the rest a that turk....uh, eagle? Then we can get out there an' see what there is to see."

Jim said sadly, "Wal, friend Jasper, they ain' no bit a thet eagle lef. Ah caught that thar bar a eatin' the last leetle bit a it. Got me mad, it did. Ah kicked him in he rear end." He looked thoughtful. "Yu reckon thet be why he wuz a chasin' me?"

"You kicked the bear?" Jasper asked in amazement.

"Wal, an' ah did, neighbor Jasper. Ah uz froze fer nourishment, ah wuz. An' thar wuz that ol' bar a eatin' our eagle. Ah tell yu, friend Jasper, it be a scandal, don' it?" After Jasper didn't answer right away, mostly because he was taken speechless by the concept of Jims kicking the large bear, Jim supplied his own answer, "It do be." This last was delivered firmly and dismissively.

Finally Jasper walked by Jim to where he'd left his pack to see if the bear had bothered it. There hadn't been anything in the pack that should have interested the bear. The only thing edible had been the turkey which had been on top.

It was as he had anticipated. The pack had not been disturbed. Jasper sank down beside it. He could have used some of the turkey himself. The only thing edible, or in this case, drinkable was the small canteen of water. Jasper had a drink and then used a small portion trying to wash the elk droppings from his beard before passing it to Jim. Getting stomped on so grieviously had taken the starch out of him.

"Maybe we orta try ta hunt somepin'. Yore stick float that d'rection, friend Jasper? Ah'm sho froze fer nourishment."

Jasper just sat for a few minutes more. He was depressed by the events of the past few minutes and he knew that he had to pull himself out of it. Sighing, he allowed, "I guess we might's well, Jim. Why don' we do it while we're going along. We need to go out there and see what's what 'bout them tracks."

Jim began to check his rifle out. "Ah'll jus' be shore muh ol' gun heah is fitten to shoot. Nevah know but whut we mought see somepin' rat close." He turned and regarded Jasper sternly. "Ah'll thank yu though, neighbor Jasper, to check whut yu have me to shoot nex' time." He hesitated a moment looking thoughtful before continuing, "Ah will say though, that thar eagle was mighty tasty." He smacked his lips in memory.

They both quartered the clearing. Jasper was becoming more dejected by the moment. As far as he could see, there had been nothing here but elk and a bear. There were no horse tracks at all. His back and chest hurt where he'd been stepped on. Finally, he just sat down and easing his pack down, leaned against it.

There was no more than a couple of hours of daylight left and Jasper seemed to have no energy to use it. He idly contemplated the problem of where they might be in relation to the meadow where he'd last seen Genevieve and the rangers. He believed that it was no more than several miles straight across in a northerly direction. The trouble was, he knew that he couldn't go straight across. There had to be several deep canyons between where he was and where they'd been. Add to that the detours necessary when cliffs or inpenetrable thickets of brush and trees barred the way and it was hard to tell how many actual miles away he was.

He was still fairly deep into contemplation of this problem when Jim called to him. "Friend Jasper, ah fount 'em. Ta tracks, thet is. They be rat heah. Come an' see."

Jasper was in a kind of deep depression and he gave Jim no more than a cursory glance before sinking back to his thoughts.

Jim was insistant though. "Friend Jasper, rat heah they be. Come along now." Jasper frowned as he looked. Jim was about a hundred feet away and he was bent over at the waist as he moved along in a northerly direction. Could he actually have found something? It wasn't likely, but he was moving in the right direction. He had to pull himself out of the depression he found himself mired in. With a mighty effort and a deep sigh, he got to his feet and slung the pack to his shoulders. He moved after Jim.

"What did ya find, Jim?" He asked as he came up.

"Wal, now yu jus' look rat chere, friend Jasper."

Jasper moved over and contemplated what Jim was looking at. There was a beaten trail heading the same direction that Jim had just been going. There were horse tracks there. The first jubilation that Jasper felt was rapidly deflated as he realized that the tracks had to be pretty old. They had been rained on and the last rain that Jasper could remember was at least a couple of weeks ago. He started to tell Jim and then bit back his words. He didn't want to hurt his feelings. Jim was here just to help Jasper, not for anything that would help himself. Besides the tracks headed in the general direction that Jasper wanted to go. He believed the trail that the rangers had been on was that direction. Why not follow the tracks, at least as long as they kept going the direction he wanted to go. It was fairly likely that this trail would go on and connect up with the main trail that the rangers would have taken.

"Good job Jim. Le's jus' foller along, what ya say?"

"Wal, thet thar suits me rat down ta the groun'. Ah'll be a huntin' as we go too. Need somepin ta eat 'fore dark."

By sundown, they'd made no more than five or six miles. They'd moved fairly slowly, mostly to spare the stiffness in Jaspers body caused by being run over, once by Jim, twice by the unwelcome bear. The only thing they'd found to eat was a few edible roots of some plants that Jasper had spotted. Getting them had been kind of slow work and Jim had grumbled about the time taken for it as cutting into his hunting time. He felt that the plants were certainly not for him to eat, saying that Jasper was robbing the animals of their rightful food.

When they stopped for the night beside a grassy seep that gathered into a small pool. Jasper thankfully took the opportunity to wash his beard thoroughly. The elk droppings didn't seem to have the same lingering powers as had the horse droppings, but he was very glad to be rid of them.

Jasper washed the roots that he'd gathered and divided them with Jim. Jim held them up and regarded them skeptically. "These yere leetle 'taters sho' ain' much fer a hongry man lak me." He watched Jasper eating his with obvious enjoyment, before finally trying a small bite of his own. "This yere turn'p sho' don' shine, ta muh way a thinkin'." He said with a grimace.

"Well Jim, it's the only thing we seen. I kinda wish you'd a seen another eagle muh self." He said with a grin.

Jim didn't take it as the joke Jasper meant it to be. "Friend Jasper, ah tell yu now, ah'm glad ah din' see no eagle. Froze as ah is fer meat, ah mount a shot one jus' in defense a muh need fer nourishment."

Contemptuous of the roots or not, Jim ate them and afterwords seemed to forget his hunger, for the moment anyhow. They spent some time on desultory conversation. Both were dead tired from the day though, and not long after dark came, they were deep asleep.

The next day about midmorning, Jim got a shot at a rabbit at long range, which he missed. This was the only thing they saw during the morning, even though Jasper kept a sharp eye out for edible plants. Jim sulked for a time after missing the rabbit, but was soon his old self, pointing things out to Jasper and telling stories of the surrounding country.

About midafternoon, they came to the top of a ridge where the trail fell away in a series of switchbacks to a deep canyon below. This was about the place where Jasper thought the trail that the rangers had been on would be.

Just past a fold of canyon a couple of miles to the east, Jasper glimpsed a lake. "Jim, looka there. You know what that there lake is?"

Jim looked at the lake and then at the surrounding country. "Mus' be thet thar's Stone Lake. Ah fis's thar f'um time ta time." He hesitated before adding, "Mounty fan fis'n' thar, it be, neighbor Jasper. Ya got eny fis'n' lan'?"

"Well, I got some line an' a few lures." He considered. He would hate to stop his hunt for the rangers, but if Jim didn't get something to eat before long, he might just revolt. "Why don' we get on down there an' see 'bout catching some fer dinner?"

"Thet be a fan idee thar, friend Jasper. Ah'll jus' lead off." With no more ado, Jim led off down the switchbacked trail.

Thirty minutes later, the trail they were on made a confluence with the more deeply beaten trail that obviously followed the larger canyon up to the lake.

Jasper moved quickly up to the trail and checked for tracks. He found them in far too large a number for him to tell what he was looking at. He squatted there scratching his head and trying to figure what he was seeing.

Jim had squatted to check them too. "Buncha hosses been thru heah, friend Jasper."

"Yeah. But are they the right ones?" Jasper responded morosely. "You make anythin' of 'em Jim? Can ya tell if them there rangers went through here? Or Genevieve?" He finished belatedly.

Jim went to his hands and knees and peered at the trail. He took so long that Jasper forgot about him and began trying to figure out what they should do. Finally Jim opined, "Friend Jasper, They be a buncha tracks heah. Ah do b'lieve though that they is tracks a them thar rangers heah. We need ta git on up thar to thet lake an' git a fu fis'. Mount be them thar rangers is up thar they own se'fes. Lot a them ol' boys come in heah sayin' they is doin' they b'iness, an' all they do is fis' an' carry on."

Jasper considered what Jim had said. There was certainly every possibility that the tracks of the rangers were here. It certainly wasn't beyond the realm of possibility either that Jim might be right about them being camped at the lake and fishing there.

"Alright Jim, le's get on up there an' find out if we can catch a few fish." And try to find those rangers, he added to himself.

The trail was good and no more than thirty minutes later, they dropped their packs on the shore. This seemed to be a fairly good sized lake for the high mountain country. Jasper thought that he could probably see two or three miles up the canyon to the farthest shore. It was, of course, not nearly that wide, being no more than a half to three quarters of a mile that way. Wooded hills rose steeply from all sides except from the upper end, where it appeared there were some small meadows and some flatter ground before rising in mountain slopes.

It was as pretty a place as Jasper had ever seen. Jim wasn't as appreciative of the view though. "Friend Jasper, do yu got that thar fis'in' lan an geah?"

Jasper smiled and gently shook his head as he dug to the bottom of the pack for the small plastic box of fishing gear. He quietly mused that he'd packed this box for the last several years as insurance against being caught in a situation that he'd need it. He was in no way fond of fish, and so far had never been in a fix where he'd been tempted to use the gear to catch himself some food. Now though, the idea didn't seem half bad. He acknowledged that he must be really hungry.

While Jim was over trying to catch supper, Jasper thought he'd just climb the slope behind them for a ways to see if he could spot anyone else that might be camped further up the lake. He hadn't climbed far when he heard Jim hollering. He kept climbing, hoping that the yelling was in celebration of catching something. Finally coming to an area of slide rock that was clear of trees and underbrush, he was able to get a look. On a small meadow close to the top of the lake, he spied horses. They were at least two miles away, probably a little further, and for that reason, nothing more than the fact that they were horses was discernable. In fact, he couldn't have sworn that they were actually horses. He acknowledged that they could very easily be elk instead. The thing that bothered him was the count. He could see that there were six of whatever was up there.

If these were indeed horses, then they couldn't be the rangers. Even with the addition of Genevieve, they'd only had four animals. Could they have found some more horses? A much more likey situation was that they'd simply met someone else that was camped on the lake fishing. Of course that was assuming that what he saw wasn't elk, or if they were horses, that they simply had nothing to do with the rangers. He sighed. There was just no way to know except to go up there and see.

He glanced at the sun, which was no more than thirty minutes from going down. By the time he got back to the camp and packed up his gear, there was no possibility of getting up there in time to snoop around and see what could be done.

The dark night would be a good time to get Genevieve back alright, but he'd need daylight to get the lay of the country in mind. Otherwise, he'd just be blundering around in the brush and trees. Probably fall over a cliff or some such, was his thought.

No, better to go back and see if Jim had caught some fish. Cook them up and then be ready to go in the morning. He was already on his way down the mountain side as those thoughts settled in his mind.

Jim was sitting in camp looking glum. "Didn' ya have no luck Jim?"

"Ah got aholt a big un. Giant beaver, he were. Took off wif all muh lan." He finished with an agrieved shake of his head.

Jasper was confused. "A beaver yuh say? A beaver took your line?"

"Wal, that were jus' a manner a speakin'. It were a fis', rat 'nough. Big ol' fis' done took muh lan. An' me froze fer nourishment." He shook his head sadly.

"Well, don' worry 'bout it Jim. Maybe we'll see something to shoot." He glanced at the sun which at that moment disappeared behind the western mountains. "Well, in the mornin' anyhow." He finished.

Jim reached behind him as he said. "Ah caught a couple 'fore thet big beaver done me in." He rather shamefacedly showed Jasper a couple of trout that were no more than six inches long.

"Hey Jim, them there fish'll taste just fine. le's start a fire an' git 'em cookin'."

Thus encouraged, Jim perked up. "Wal, they be beaver, in a kinda way enyhow, ain' they?"

Jasper clapped him on the shoulder by way of answer as he hurried away for firewood.

Chapter Ten

He told Jim of what he'd seen at the lakes upper end while they ate the fish. Jims first reaction was to get on up there. "Why, we mought can steal some a they food, serve 'em rat too, it would. Astealin' yu hoss lak they done did." He finshed righteously.

Jim was as tired as Jasper though, and it took little argument to convince him that they should wait until morning. They sat by the fire and Jim began a story of panning some gold over east aways, but it got mixed up in a dream as Jasper started to snore.

They were up and moving early. Jim had suggested hunting for something for breakfast, but he saw the sense of Jaspers argument that if the rangers were indeed camped further up the lake, it would be hard to explain away any shooting. That didn't, however, deter Jim from nearly continuous grumbling of which Jasper only caught an occassional "Hongry".

When they got close to the lake top, Jasper suggested climbing the mountain slope at least high enough to get an idea, if possible, of where the rangers might be camped. He got Jim to go along with the idea by promising to be on the lookout for some kind of edible plant. Although he'd professed not to be fond of the roots that Jasper had found the other day, he was now hungry enough to eat anything. At least thats how he put it.

From a small clearing a couple of hundred feet up the mountain slope, they spied a tendril of smoke from a campfire. It was another half mile up and close to the lake. Although he'd found nothing for Jim to eat, the actual sight of the smoke from the campfire seemed to give Jim purpose. He seemed to forget his hunger and after staring in the direction of where Jasper pointed out the smoke, Jasper had to wonder whether Jim could actually see it, he said, "Friend Jasper, yu don' got much 'perience 'bout this yere kinda thang. Ah bettah injun on in thar an' see whuts whut. Whyn't yu jus' kinda hang back 'n ah'll come git yuh when ah fin' out 'bout thangs?"

Jasper had no intention of just hanging back and letting Jim wander in there alone. But he didn't want to dull the enthusiasm that Jim was showing either, or have him remember his hunger. "Alright Jim. You go on along. I'll jus' mosey that way so you don't have to come far back to find me."

Jim beamed. "Fan idee, Friend Jasper. Ah'll jus' go on 'long then. Find whicha way they stick be a floatin', yu bet." The thick beard and whiskers swept to the side in a nod.

Jasper let him get out of sight before moving that way himself. He moved off to the side a little and then made his way straight at the last place he'd seen the smoke. He began to think he'd missed it when he came to the edge of a small clearing. He stopped behind the cover of a spruce tree and peeked around the edge. There was a tent there alright. Matter of fact, there were three tents. Jasper scratched his head. Was it possible the rangers had three tents? He doubted it. They'd only had one set of pack boxes, and these were good sized tents. He doubted the tents alone would have fit in the pack boxes he'd seen, let alone the other things necessary for an extended camping trip.

It was then that his attention was drawn to a movement. He had to peek further around the tree to see what it was. Seated on a log by the campfire was a woman. He ducked back. What was a woman doing here? One thing for sure, there'd been no woman with them when he'd last seen the rangers. He glanced at the sun. It was probably around eight. It had taken them at least a couple of hours to get this far. Shaking his head slightly, he peeked again. It was a sure enough real live woman. She appeared to be sitting there drinking coffee, or at least something from a cup.

Stretching further, he was able to see that she appeared to be the only one in camp, unless someone else might be in one of the tents. There was no sound from them though and he dismissed the idea as unlikely.

He took a moment to wonder what had become of Jim. That thought was quickly submerged in another thought. The rangers, while certainly not in evidence at the moment, still might be camped here with this party. He knew that he'd have to go in and ask some questions, but first he needed to know where Jim was. It would be embarrassing to be asking questions and have Jim come blundering in at that time. He'd just have to find Jim before they went in.

He slipped back aways through the timber before moving over the direction that Jim had taken. He began to watch for tracks, trying to find out if Jim had crossed here. He'd gone about a hundred yards without seeing anything when he stopped by a thick bush to look and listen. Without warning, something leaped from the bush and grabbing Jasper around the middle, threw him violently to the ground.

A voice came close to his ear, "Ah got yu fair n' squar mist' rangah. Now, is yu gon' tell me whar muh frien's hoss is, Er do ah gotta git mean wif yu?"

Jasper was totally befuddled. His breath was partially knocked away and he was disoriented by the sudden attack. In spite of all that though, there was no mistaking Jims voice. "Jim," he gasped out, "What is it that you're doin'?"

Jim loosed his hold and grabbing Jaspers shoulder, turned him partly over, he peered closely into Jaspers face before asking, "Be that yu, Friend Jasper? Whut yu adoin' heah? Ah thought yu wuz one them thar ranger mens."

Jasper was getting his breath back and with it came irritation. It seemed to be getting a habit to be run over and thrown down by Jim. Along with an assortment of bears and what have you. "Dog--gone it Jim, What is it that you're doin'. Even if I had been a ranger, we can't be tacklin' 'em an' throwin' 'em down. We're supposed to be sneaky 'bout this, don' ya know?"

"Wal, neighbor Jasper," Jim said helping him to his feet. "Ah were a hidin' rat thar, an' when he, that is when yu, stopped, ah thought ah'd been found out. So ah jus' thought ah'd throw 'im down and git the wharbouts a yo' hoss. We could git her an' git gone fore anybuddy knowed we 'uz even 'round 'bout heah. Leasyways that thars how ah figgered it."

From his tone, Jasper figured that under all the hair, Jim must have had a hangdog expression. He sighed, rubbing an arm which had taken quite a thump on the way down, "Well, don' worry about it Jim. You was just doin' your best, I know that." Remembering the camp, he said, "Look, I found their camp over there about a hundred or so yards. Have you seen anything of horses or anyone at all?"

"Naw. Ah wuza injunin' along slow an' easy when ah heared yu acomin along. Ah ain' seen nothin' else."

"Well, le's get over to the camp. They don' seem to be nobody there except some woman settin' by the fire."

"Nobody thar 'ceptin' a womans? Whut yu reckon she be adoin' thar by she se'f, friend Jasper?"

Jasper stopped and turned to face him. "I don' know. It might be that them rangers is camped with 'em. There is three tents there, anyhow. If it is them there, they could be off doin' 'bout anything. course, if it's somone else an' not the rangers at all, they'd pro'bly be off fishing this time a morning." He rubbed his chin reflectively. "I can't figure nothin' else, anyway."

Jim considered this for a minute before nodding. "Ah s'pose yu mus' be rat, friend Jasper. If yu is, though, how we go'n fand out 'bout it?"

"Well, I was thinkin' on it. Them rangers don' know I exist. You mighta met 'em a time or two, but you said you hadn't had trouble with them, so as long as we just go in like any others that are up here to fish, or whatever, we should be able to ask some questions without gettin' their suspicions up."

After a moments consideration of what Jasper had said, Jim gave a noncommittal shrug. "Ah s'pose thet's sense a'right. Le's go in an' see how they stick is afloatin'. Mought be, they is got somepin to eat in thar too."

Well, at least Jim's back to normal, thinking of his stomach, was Jaspers thought as they moved toward the campsite. He stopped as they reached the clearing edge. The woman was still where she'd been, just sitting and staring at the campfire. Occassionally, she'd take a sip from the cup in her hands.

Jasper stopped and in a tone calculated to carry to her but not much further, hollered, "Hello, the camp."

It was his intention to alert her so she wouldn't be startled as they walked up. It didn't work. She started so violently that the liquid in her cup splashed high in the air and seemed to mostly come down on her. She looked down at herself with a disgusted expression, before turning to them with most of that expression still intact.

Jasper inspected her as she turned, she seemed to be nice looking, although maybe just a bit beyond pleasantly plump. "Hope we didn't scare you ma'am." Jasper courteously intoned.

She looked at him for a moment before turning her attention to Jim. "Heh, heh, heh." She giggled. It was Jaspers turn to be started at the high girlish trill. "Why, you mighta startled me just a little, but that's ok. Come on in and have a seat." She simpered, ducking her head coyly.

There was another log across the fire and it was there that she indicated for them to sit. Jasper was halfway there when something made him look over his shoulder at Jim. He was just standing there and although nothing could be seen of his expression because of the hair, Jasper could see from his motionless staring attitude that something was amiss.

Moving quickly back, he whispered, "Something wrong with you Jim?" He took Jims arm and shook it slightly.

Jim seemed to come out of it a bit. He swung his head to regard Jasper as if he'd never before seen him, "Uh.....Whut's thet yu asayin' neighbor?....uh..."

"Jasper. Whats wrong with you Jim. Don' you know my names Jasper?"

"Uh..Jasper. rat." He said vaguely, his attention clearly swinging back to the woman that was standing and looking at them curiously now.

"Dog--gone it Jim, we gotta get in there an' ask some questions. Buck up now." Again he shook Jims arm.

This time Jim came out of it a little more. He seemed to have some intelligence in the eyes behind the thick lens. "Uh...Yeah, neighbor Jasper. Whut is it thet yu're a wantin'?"

Grateful that Jim seemed to be back from whereever, Jasper pulled him along as he whispered, "Come on, we gotta get up there and ask our questions."

Jim seemed to be back all the way now. "Oh, rat. Rat. Ah tell yu friend Jasper, lemme do the talkin'," he said in a whisper that could have been heard at the other end of the lake. That suggestion mightily alarmed Jasper, who had seen little that Jim had done to make him confident that he'd be able to find anything out that they wanted to know without making the woman suspicious. But since Jim had quickly moved ahead, stopping him with anything short of a open field tackle seemed unlikely.

Jasper hurried after, but he stopped open mouthed with amazement as the backcountry bumpkin acting hairy Jim swept low in a bow. At the same time he grabbed his head as if to doff a nonexistent hat. Since no hat was there, he succeeded only in jerking out a handfull of hair, causing him to jerk upright in pain. He covered that blunder beautifully though, nonchalantly tossing the hair aside as he intoned, "Mah deah, Ah has the pleashuh to be Jim Bridger. An' this yere is Jasper..Ah..Jasper. Whut be yore name friend Jasper?" He turned his head to ask Jasper as he shielded his mouth with a hand. Again, anyone could have heard him at a half a mile.

Jasper whispered back, "What's the matter with you Jim. You know my names Caine. Jasper Caine." He repeated in exasperation.

Jim swung back to the woman, "Oh rat, rat. Jasper Caine. An' whut mought be yo' name, mah deah?"

The large woman covered her mouth with a hand as she giggled, "Heh, heh, heh. I'm Millie. Millie Jones." She looked around as though she'd just now arrived, finally gesturing to the log. "Won't you gent'men sit down?"

When they were seated, Millie asked, "You're kind of old, aren't you Jim? Heh, heh, heh."

Jim appeared taken aback. "Whut is it thet yu mean, Millie mah deah?"

"Well, heh, heh, heh, I read that Jim Bridger was born along about the early eighteen hundreds. Heh, heh, heh."

Jims guffaws lasted longer than the joke deserved. Jasper politely joined in with a weak and brief "Ha, ha."

"Thas a gud wun, Millie mah deah. Yu is got a fine sense a fun, isn't yu?" The hairy head seemed to positively vibrate with his sense of the presence of the lady.

"Well, heh, heh, heh. I try." She sobered as she looked around. "It gets kind of lonesome just sitting here." There was a shine in her eye as she again looked at them. But not precisely at them, it was mostly just at Jim.

Jim immediately leaned forward in sympathy. "Lonesome? Why be thet, mah deah? How long is yu bin heah?"

Millie took a sip from her cup as she took a moment to consider the question. Jasper had to wonder what was in her cup if she took this long to answer something so simple, especially since her answer was what it was when it came. "I guess we been here two days. Yes, two days is what it is." She finished positively.

This information made even Jim draw back a bit in puzzlement. "Ah, well Millie, whut fer you come up yere ennyhow? Air yu by yusef?"

"Oh no. Heh, heh, heh. I'd be scared to be here by myself. I came along with my sister and brother-in-law. Oh, and a wrangler," she finished belatedly as if she'd nearly forgotten him.

Both Jim and Jasper swung their heads to look at the tents. "Are they in the tents?" asked Jasper.

"Oh no. Heh, heh, heh. They're all off fishing."

"You didn't come up here to fish?" asked Jasper.

Millie sighed. "Well, I did, but I can't stand those wiggly fish. The first one I caught was my last. I can eat them, but I'm not going to catch them any more." She finished positively.

At this Jim gallantly got up and bowed again. "Nary a reason in the worl' thet yu shud, Millie mah deah. Yu is a lady, ah kin tell jus' bah lookin'."

Millie got up and moved around bashfully. "Heh, heh, heh. Oh Jim, how you do go on. Heh, heh, heh." Jim wheeled around to keep facing her.

Jasper shook his head and looked at the ground in sad astonishment. He'd never seen anything like it, he thought. Looks like a couple of Clydesdales prancing around, he mused maliciously. Well, he thought that he knew one way to get Jims attention. "Uh.. ma'am, you wouldn't have some little bit of food you could maybe sell us, would you. We kind of ran short an' we been goin' kinda skimpy lately." He explained.

"Oh, are you boys hungry? My goodness, where are my manners. Theres some biscuits left over here in the dutch oven. And then there's some bacon that was left too, this morning. If that's alright, it's right here by the fire. We can always cook some eggs and some other things too."

Jaspers astonishment was total when Jim said, "Why, Millie mah deah, we ain' much hongry. Don' yu put yuse'f no way out." But he quickly restored Jaspers faith when he added, "But since yu is offerin', why ah allow as to how we cud eat some a them thar biscuts and bacon."

Jim ate like he was starved. There was a lot there too. Someone must have thought they'd have a lot of hungry people that morning. That or maybe no one had been hungry and that was why they hadn't eaten much of what was there. As they'd got their plates full and sat down on the log to eat, Millie had filled two cups from the coffee pot and handed one to each of them. Tipping the cup up to wash a large mouthful of bacon and biscuits down, Jasper took a long drink. Suddenly fire seemed to fill his mouth. He couldn't breath and ended up coughing explosively, spraying food. It was a long minute before he was finally breathing good enough that he felt he could talk again.

"What was that?" He gasped, although he recognized the taste of the whiskey and knew that's what it was.

Jim was regarding him with puzzlement. He'd taken a big drink and it hadn't seemed to faze him. "Air somepin wrong wif yu, neighbor Jasper?"

Millie was giggling her high pitched giggle. “Isn't my coffee to your liking, mister Caine?”

Still gasping, Jasper croaked, “What is that you got in that there coffee?”

With another simpering giggle, Millie answered, “Oh, just a little anesthetic to help me stand it up here. Heh, heh, heh.”

“Why, thet's a mighty fan joke, Millie mah deah. Ah do b'lieve that this yere is fan coffee.” He emptied his cup and extended it for a refill.

Jasper took a cautious sip. He thought he'd spit all of the previous drink out, but some must have gone down because this drink tasted far better than the last one had. Sipping occasionally, he finished his plate of food. Surprising himself, he found that he had his cup extended for a refill. It tasted mighty good by now.

Jim and Millie were laughing and cutting up and telling stories by the time Jasper had finished that cup of coffee and whiskey. He was surprised to find that his lips were kind of numb. Suddenly, he realized that he was getting drunk and that wasn't what he was supposed to be doing.

Interrupting a story that Jim had begun to tell, he asked Millie, “We're lookin' for a couple of rangers that mighta come by here. You know, fellers that woulda been in uniform. Any fellers like that been by here?”

His voice didn't sound just right to him and Millie didn't act as though she fully understood what he'd said. He wasn't at all sure whether that was because of what he'd had to drink or what she'd earlier drank. She finally figured it out though, and answered, “I do believe that there was a couple of people through here in uniform.” She turned to Jim and confided, “I do so admire men in uniform.”

Jim preened a little, “Wal Millie mah deah, ah has allas looked on this yere buckskin suit ah got, as a kinda uniform. Kinda like the chief a ta mountain men, don' ya know?”

Millie preened, “Heh, heh, heh. Why I thought that you looked like a soldier all the time Jim. That rifle gun you got looks nice on you too. Heh, heh, heh.”

Jim would have made some answer but Jasper cut in. "What happened to them rangers? Are they camped around here somewhere?"   Millie seemed to be a trifle fuzzy and slow in her thinking and it took some time to unravel that question. Finally she answered uncertainly, "I think they were going on further into the mountains. I wasn't paying much attention though. They were only here for long enough to have a cup of coffee with Jeff." At the puzzled expression in Jaspers eye, she explained. "Jeff Slien. That's my brother-in-law. They came through here yesterday at noon. No, wait. I think it was two days ago. It was just after we got here a while. Yeah, it must have been then. Jeff was here at noon and he talked to them. I do believe though, that I overheard the rangers say that they were going up into the mountains for something." She hesitated as she tried to remember. Finally, she shrugged, "I can't remember. If I even heard anything else, I've forgotten."

"Well, that's alright." Said Jasper. "Your folk'll be back for noon anyhow, won't they? We can ask them about it then."

She shook her head. "No. They went up to some creek to fish. Left way early and won't be back 'til after dark. That's what they said anyway."

Dog--gone, Jasper thought. It seems that nothing was going their way. He shook his head. There seemed to be nothing to do except wait for the brother-in-law to come back though. The only other thing that occured to him was to try to track the rangers. That appealed none at all though. He'd already had a sample of Jims tracking ability and had been less than impressed with it. He acknowledged his own deficiency in that area too. No, their best bet would be to wait and get a definite direction to follow along. That decided, he cut into the flirtatious conversation of the other two, "Millie, we need to wait and ask your brother-in-law about where them rangers was goin'. Do you mind if we wait here? We could go back to our camp and wait there for them if you'd rather."

Millie had just given Jim another refill of coffee and whiskey, and since she was standing she attempted a pirouette as she turned back to Jasper. She seemed to be light on her feet and in a sober condition, she might have succeeded. Now though, her balance was impaired from the spiked coffee and as she turned, she lost her balance and fell sideways into Jim. Jim was busy taking a large drink of his refilled coffee and so wasn't ready to catch her. So it was that she knocked him backwards over the log he was sitting on. The coffee spilled and Jim landed on his back. Befuddled by whiskey, he lay on there as helpless as an overturned beetle. The resemblance to a beetle was enhanced too, by his arms and legs futilely waving in the air.

When Millie bounced off Jim, she then fell full length across the fire. The fire hadn't been big to start with and it had mostly burned down, but Millie's slacks immediately began to smoke. With what was for Jasper a superhuman effort, he jumped forward and picked Millie up in his arms and carrying her in a hunched staggering walk, he headed for the lake. It was only about twenty feet away and when he got there, there was a small cliff some four or five feet high. The trouble was that Jaspers view of the water was blocked by Millie's bulk so that instead of stopping and dropping Millie in to quench any fire she might have on her clothes, as had been his firm intention, he ran right off the cliff and both of them plunged under the water.

The water was icy and Jasper came up blowing. He immediately looked around for Millie and observed that she'd been more fortunate that he himself and had landed close to the bank. She was already climbing out. She turned and he swam over for her to help him out. This she did, but as soon as he was on the bank and standing, she hauled off and slapped him so hard that he flew backwards off the bank to land in the lake again.

When he came to the surface, he was somewhat fuzzy in his thinking, but not fuzzy enough to try to get out anywhere close to Millie. He swam several yards down to a low rock to get out this time. He resembled nothing so much as a drowned rat when he finally stood on dry ground again. Millie advanced on him again with what he deduced was a measure of fire in her eye. "What'd you throw me in the lake for?" If she'd raised her voice one more decibel in volume, it would have been a scream.

Jasper held out both hands, palm forward. "Don't ya remember fallin' in the fire? Your slacks was smokin', an I thought I needed to get you in the water right away."

"Oh yeah. I look like I needed to be put in the water, Don't I?" She said, loudly sarcastic.

Jasper was still befuddled by being in the lake twice, as well as the slap that had been backed the considerable bulk and muscle of Millie. Something nevertheless occurred to him and he hoped it proved out. "Miss Millie, check your slacks there. They was a smoking right enough. They musta been scorched."

She continued looking him in the eye for a moment with that disbelieving frown before looking down at her slacks. The front showed nothing of any scorching, that much Jasper could see from where he stood. She twisted to look at the back of them and as she did, her look changed. With a stricken expression, she twisted the slacks to show a large blackened place. There were two or three small holes burned in the material too.

She turned back to him. "Oh Jasper, I'm so ashamed. You saved me." She started for him with her arms spread wide.

Jasper backed up in alarm. He wasn't at all sure which he prefered, the slap he'd endured or the threatened embrace. He quickly fended her off. "It wasn't nothin' miss Millie. Don' give it another thought."

"Well I'm just so ashamed. I hit you too. Oh, please forgive me."

Jasper was saved from more embarrassment at that point by the timely arrival of Jim, who had finally got rolled over and had succeeded in regaining his feet. He peered closely at Millie. "Why whut be it that yu been adoin', Millie mah deah? It don' noways seem hot 'nough to be sweatin' like that thar. You reckon yu feelin' good?"

Chapter Eleven

Jims bulk was blocking Millies sight of Jasper as she said, "Why, Jasper saved my life. I was burning up and he....." Jasper didn't hear the rest of the conversation as he'd taken advantage of the diversion of the Jims timely arrival to head off into the brush. He figured that the explanations ought to take long enough to let him get out of sight.

He went at least a mile before finding a place to his liking. It was a large fairly flat rock that the sun was shining brightly on and thick foliage grew all around. He was shivering mightily in his wet clothes and he lost no time in stripping and spreading them out to dry. The sun was warm on the rock and he took advantage of the clothes drying time to toast and take a long nap.

It was past noon when he woke. The sun was hot on the rock and he was glad to put on the still slightly wet clothes and leave. The buckskin shirt in particular was damp and clammy, but he put it on anyway as he moved off.

Now that he was awake and thinking about it, he wished that he hadn't left Jim there at the camp. He had a bad feeling about Jim being drunk and wobbling around as he'd been doing. There was no telling what kind of trouble that Jim was capable of getting into in the state he'd been in when Jasper had left the camp.

About half way back, he thought he heard something. He stopped and cocked an ear. There was definitely something there. It seemed to be an eerie ululation reminding him of nothing so much as the howling of a wolf. Although he'd never heard a wolf howl, he thought it would have to sound like what he was hearing. While he listened, the sound died and wasn't repeated. When he moved on ahead, the brush was thicker and so noisy to move through that he doubted that he'd have heard it even if it started again. The uncertainty of whether it might indeed be a wolf close by was a little unnerving though.

It was when he got closer to the camp that unusual and unnatural sounds became definitely audible. He stopped and listened. There was more of the wolf sounds, although seemingly more muted than before. There was also another sound that he couldn't place at all. It was a high pitched "Eh, he, eh" that was repeated at a more or less random interval. From time to time, there was also a chittering gibbering sound. Moving through the gloom of the thick trees as Jasper was now doing, these noises had him feeling just a little nervous and spooky.

It was only when he reached the edge of the camp clearing that the mystery was cleared up. He stood and watched in astonishment as Jim danced. The mystery of the wolf call was cleared up too as Jim put his hand to his mouth to produce the classic indian ululation or war cry.

Jim was dancing with a mighty effort that had sweat streaming off his face. The other noises were revealed at this time also. Millie was sitting on one of the logs dressed in different and much drier clothes than the last time Jasper had seen her. She was cheering Jim on, sometimes with high pitched squeals, but mostly with shrill giggles. The amazing thing was that Jim wasn't doing any indian kind of dance which would have fit in with his mountain man penchant for all things. It seemed to Jasper that what he was doing was a kind of twist dance, mixed in with maybe a lot of the other screwy modern dances.

Jasper stood there feeling dismal and inadequate. He knew that he should probably move on in and try to get Jim to take it a little easy. The durn fool was liable to take a heart attack if he kept it up, but he doubted that Jim would listen. It seemed that most everything that they did in the way of trying to get Genevieve back had backfired on them. And now Jim over there drunk and making a fool of himself. If he kept it up, he'd more than likely be too sick tomorrow to help much, even assuming that Millies folks gave them adequate directions to where the rangers had gone.

Shaking his head sadly, he turned and moved back to a tree that was out of sight of the clearing and the rowdy Jim. Slumping to the ground, he pulled his hat over his eyes and relaxed. Gradually the noise from the clearing faded as he dozed.

Something woke him. It took a minute to sink in that something was different. Then it hit. The noise had ceased. There was nothing but silence. This though, was not reassuring. Jim had been making far too much noise to just quit entirely. As Jasper jumped up and headed for the clearing, he had a bad feeling.

As he came to the clearing edge, Jim was revealed laying by one of the seating logs by the fire. He'd evidently tripped over it as he was laying at right angles. Millie was standing next to him peering down into his face. She was swaying so much that Jasper started to run forward, afraid she'd fall on the prostrate Jim. Just as he moved forward though, she staggerd off to one of the tents and entered.

Jasper slowed his approach a little, while still hurrying. He thought that Jim still might have had the heart attack that he'd earlier worried about. He was still some little way off though when he heard Jim give a mighty snore. The rest of the approach was made at a slower and much more disgusted pace. A quick check showed that Jim had done nothing more than pass out in a drunken sleep. Jasper broke a couple of branches from a nearby bush and put them over Jims face to shade him some.

He wondered if Millie was alright and moved to the tent that she'd gone in. As he approached, he heard snores that rivaled those of Jim and he detoured to the lake edge to sit there and watch the lake and feel sorry for himself as he waited for dark and the return of Millies party.

He roused himself about an hour before dark with the thought that Millies brother-in-law and sister might be more than just a little disgusted if they came in and found Jim and Millie laying around in a drunked up sleep. While he thought that the two deserved some trouble for what they'd done, he didn't want that trouble to extend to making Millies folks too disgusted to tell him about the rangers. While that eventuality might be unlikely, he decided to take no chances.

He went to Jim and shook him. Surprisingly, it took little shaking to wake Jim up and after he'd got up and shook himself off a bit, he seemed not too much the worse for wear. This amazed Jasper, but it was something that he was grateful for. He sent Jim to wake up Millie. Jasper himself was more than just a little leery of startling her in any way. He kept wiggling a tooth with his tongue that felt just bit loose from her very hefty slap of this morning.

It took some loud yells from Jim before Millie came to the tent flap. She was clearly not in any kind of good shape. Her face appeared kind of squashed and she couldn't seem to open her eyes to the glare of day. After just a moment, she turned and reentered the tent. Jim shrugged and came to the fire where they both sat disconsolately, wondering what they should do.

In about five minutes, Millie solved their problems. She reappeared looking every bit as bright as she had that morning. The change in her appearance totally confused Jasper for a minute before the answer came to him. She must have had some hair of the dog. A bit more of the whiskey to set her up. That had to be the answer. She asked them to build the fire up a bit, which they hurried to do.

She went to the pack box and in just a few minutes, she had coffee on and was opening cans for a supper. When she asked Jim a little later if he'd like a drink, he surprised Jasper by declining. Jasper was beginning to feel good about things again. If they got a good steer to where the rangers had gone, they should be able to do something about it tomorrow.

It was a good hour after dark though, when they heard the sound of the horses of the returning fishermen. Jim had regained all of his good spirits and had seemed to have totally thrown off the effects of the serious drinking that he'd done earlier in the day. Jasper was very grateful for the way Millie had rallied too. She'd made several trips to the tent, which Jasper had decuced was for nips of liquor, but she'd evidently taken no more than enough to carry her along at a pleasant level.

Now as the riders came into the glow cast by the blazing camp fire, she moved confidently over to the man in the lead. "Jeff, Susan, I want you to meet Jasper and Jim. They've been keeping me company here today."

Jasper didn't know if he liked such a baldfaced way of revealing their daylong presence here. Jeff was shown in the rather dim firelight to be a medium tall man, maybe close to six feet. He was dressed in a denim jacket against the chill of the evening that did little to conceal a body that either worked out with the weights or else held a job that required considerable muscle excercise. His features were blurred by a few days growth of beard, his shaving chores evidently forgotten on this trip. His expression, at least as much as could be discerned from his eyes that appeared to be none too warm and the flat slash of his mouth did not inspire any confidence at all in regard to his good humor.

Millies sister, Susan, whose name he didn't remember hearing until just now, simply looked surprised. She was a pretty woman who appeared to be somewhat younger than Millie and much slimmer. She seemed willing to be friendly as she tried a tentative smile. Behind and barely visible at the far edge of the firelight sat the wrangler. He wore a rather ragged denim jacket and appeared to be quite skinny. A droopy wide brimmed hat shadowed his face to the point that nothing whatever could be seen of it. The firelight did however, dimly show a long gray beard that reached to his midchest.

"You boys lookin' for somethin'?" This from Jeff.

"Why Jeff, don't you think they mighta come to see me? Heh, heh heh."

Jeffs face cracked for the first time in a small grin. He must have been fond of Millie. "Yeah Millie, that thought did occur to me." He shifted his attention back to Jasper and Jim although the slight smile remained.

Jim made as if to move foreward, a move that Jasper figured he'd better forestall if he ever wanted to get any information about the rangers. He held his hand out to stop Jim while he explained. "Mister Slien, we're on the track of two rangers, or game wardens, whichever. We got some information for them and we been trying to track 'em down. Millie tells us that they came through here the other day. The reason we stopped was that she didn't remember exactly where they said they was goin' an' she thought that you might."

Jeff remained silent, just staring at him for a few moments more. Finally, he sighed and stepped down off his horse. As he turned to them, he said, "Yeah, they told me where they was going. Rangers is what they were, not game wardens, forest rangers." He finished. He seemed about to say something more, but delayed it as he turned to his wife and told her to get down. "Come an' take care of the horses, Chuck. Oh, this here's Chuck Fontis." He belatedly introduced the wrangler. For the wranglers part, he simply touched his hat with his finger by way of acknowledgement as he took the horses reins and led them away.

"That smells mighty good, Millie." Jeff said as he moved up to the fire. Millie poured him a cup of coffee, afterword doing the same thing for Susan. There was audible sighs from both as they sank down on one of the logs and sipped from their cups.

Jim had been nearly vibrating with the effort of keeping quiet and now the urge to speak grew too strong. Stepping forward, he asked, "Did yu ketch airy big beaver up to thet creek whar yu went a fis'in'?"

With a puzzled frown, Jeff asked, "Beaver? Why we wasn't fishin' for beaver. Just fish." With almost no break, he asked the thing that occurred to him. "How would you fish for beaver anyway? Is that even legal?"

"Oh no. Fis' is whut ah were a askin 'bout." Jim held his arms out and swung around to show his buckskin suit with all it's fringes. "A moun'tin man is whut ah has the pleasha to be, an us moun'tin mens allas says this is beaver an' thas beaver, mostly no mattah whut they be speakin' on. Yu unnerstan?"

Jeff had a pleasantly bemused expression on his face as he stared at Jim as though he was something that he'd never seen before, as he probably hadn't. After a false start, he answered. "Yeah, I believe

I do understand." After a another short hesitation as though he'd forgotten what it was that Jim had asked him, he belatedly answered, "Well we caught quite a bunch of fish. We only got a couple that were big enough to save though." He looked off to where the wrangler had led the horses. "As soon as Chuck gets back with our gear, I'll show them to you. Susan got one that's twenty inches long. I thought that you mighta heard about it clear down here, she was hollering so loud." he finished, laughing.

"Throwed alla them thar beaver back, air yu a sayin'?" The totally shocked tone of Jims voice made Jasper wish that he could see the others expression behind the thick beard. He had a idea that it would have been funny to see.

Jeff took a moment to stare at Jim before slowly answering, "Well, we usually don't keep many that we catch unless they're big ones. Not even then if we get more than a couple." He was obviously somewhat perplexed concerning Jim.

Jims glasses seemed to take a bead just a little to the side of Jeff, as he asked, "Whut be ta reason fer yu ta be a fis'in', if'n it don' be fer ta eat?"

At this point Susan broke in, "Why, haven't you ever fished just for fun, Jim?"

Jim stroked his beard as he thought about this. "Wal, ah mount a fis'ed fer fun jus' a leetle, but ah guess ah nevah did catch near many beaver 'fore ah got hongry an' quit fis'in fer to cook 'em and eat 'em." This little philosophical discussion out of the way, Jim cheerfully acknowledged, "Whut it be thet ah allas say though, if yu stick be a floatin' thet way 'bout ketching big beavers an' leetle ones too, wal then it be thet yo' way do sho'ly shine wif me." Jims friendly grin cracked so wide that his teeth shown white through the thick beard.

Both Susan and Jeff were sitting and staring at Jim as they couldn't quite decipher what he was saying, which Jasper figured was just exactly what was wrong with them. He broke in here, as much to spare the Sliens as to get information. "Mr. Slien, 'bout them rangers. You said you knew where they might be going. You think you could maybe steer us right so we could follow on along and catch them?"

It seemed to be with some difficulty that Jeff tore his attention from the grinning Jim and it took a moment to guide his mind to this new problem. Susan made no pretense of shifting from her examination of Jim. Her gaze may have been just a trifle apprehensive as she tried to come to terms with what it was that she was seeing and hearing.

Shaking his head slightly, Jeff finally answered, "Yeah, they said that they was going up to the Glacier Creek area to take an elk count. I believe that they said they'd be there for three or four days. Then they were going over to Jacks Creek for the same thing. I remember the names of those two creeks because I thought that if the fishing up in them was any good, we might try it, but they didn't know anything about that. Didn't seem to have any interest in fishing at all." As he fihished, his tone of voice grew puzzled, as though the disinterest of fishing by anyone was an incomprehensible thing to him.

At this point, Jim broke in with the start of a story about a big beaver, translation, fish, that he'd about caught one time somewhere. Luckily, the story got cut short by the timely arrival of Chuck. He came into the fire light carrying a set of small canvas pack bags.

Jeff motioned him over and took one of the bags. Digging down into it, he came up with a fish stringer with two very nice trout. "Look here fellers. You ever in your life seen a prettier rainbow than that." The fish on show was a pretty thing. Deep bodied with the distinctive pink rainbow on its side nearly glowing in the dim light. Jeff turned to Susan and hugged her. "I'm proud of you babe." He enthused. It was clear that the way to Jeffs heart was through catching a big fish. Jasper irrelevantly wondered if she got as much attention for other things, but that contemplation got side tracked as Jim got into the picture again.

"Thet be a fan fis'. Ah be a tellin' yu neighbor Jeff, was yu to hang thet thar fis' ovah the far, thet would be beaver what would shine. Ah'm froze fer nourishment." He smacked his lips with an audible sound.

Chapter Twelve

Susan stared at Jim with her mouth hanging open. She'd forgotten that she had a cup of coffee in her hand. Jeff too, stared helplessly. Jasper cringed. He figured that they were close to being tossed out of the camp because Jeff would have to figure that Jim was acting like a drunken fool. He had no way to realize that Jim was merely acting like Jim, and as far as Jasper had seen, was incapable of acting like anything else.

He sighed. He guessed that he'd better act as a kind of interpreter. At least that gave him a chance to try to correct the impression that Jim was mocking them. "Uh..Mister Slien, Jim was just admiring your fish. Some of that mountain man talk is kinda hard to understand until you been around it some." He looked earnestly at them.

Jeff seemed to shake himself slightly, "Uh..Yeah. Well, I think maybe I got the drift." He took a moment more to think about it, after which he seemed to get tickled. "Yeah, I do believe that you want some of this here fish to eat, is that right Jim?"

"Thet wud sho'ly shine wif me, friend Jeff an' leetle lady." He bowed to the still stupified Susan, who finally came out of it and rewarded him with a wan smile. She still had a puzzled look on her face, but she had clearly decided to just go along with things.

Jeff turned to her and asked, "Is it okay to cook your fish, honey?"

She waved a negligent assent. It seemed that she didn't want to get very closely involved until she was more sure of what was going on. If she listened close, maybe she might even begin to understand what language it was that Jim was talking.

Jim, ever helpful, said, "Why, jus lemme at that thar ol' fis'. Ah'll tek 'im down ta lake an clean 'im good."

"Well, we already cleaned him. We'll just put him in a pan and maybe we can get Millie to cook him for us?" Jeffs tone made that last a question to her.

Replying with a radiant smile at Jeff, Millie went to the pack boxes and returned with a large frying pan. While she busied herself with preparing the fish, Jim began to regale everyone with ancedotes of fish he'd caught and cooked, although he inevitably referred the fish as beaver. By now though, all had seemed to catch on to what he was talking about, although there was some confusion when a few minutes later, he began a story about a real beaver. It didn't take long though until they were just enjoying what Jim said, without giving undue attention to the terms that he used.

When Millie announced that the fish and the other things that she'd prepared were ready, Jasper used the small confusion of everyone washing up to pull Jim to the side. "You know where that Glacier Creek an' Jack Creek is at?"

"Why sho'. Ah knows 'bout 'em. Whut be it thet yu is wantin' wif 'em ennyhow, neighbor Jasper?"

Jasper pulled back slightly to look at the other. "What I want with them? Good grief, Jim. Didn't you hear Jeff say that's where them there rangers went to?"

Jim was taking small glances at the cooking fish and testing the air for smells, although, from past experience, Jasper doubted that he was getting any of the smells whatever. It did however, explain his forgetfulness of what Jeff had said of the rangers. He finally seemed to remember. "Oh rat, rat. Yeah, ah knows whar they be." He was so obviously preoccupied with the impending meal that Jasper let him go. As long as he knew where the rangers had gone and could lead Jasper to them, he was satisfied.

The meal was excellent, lent flavor as much by the setting of the lake and mountains as by the quality. Jasper couldn't fully appreciate it though. They'd lost a full day here, as well as the other days lost pursuing the trail of the elk. Even now, the rangers could be moving to Jack creek, which would put them even further behind. It was even possible that they could change their plans entirely, leaving Jasper and Jim with no idea at all of where to look.

If Jasper was uneasy and not enjoying himself fully, it was certainly not the case with Jim. He had fallen into his own here, laughing and cutting up. Telling improbable stories and jokes. It was clear that now they'd got used to him, the party was mightily taken with his antics. Each time he'd show signs of running down a bit, they'd urge him on and he'd find something else to tell them, to their delight.

One way and another, it had been a tiring day for Jasper and he figured the next for just more of the same. They'd been sitting for the best part of two hours when Jasper took advantage of a small lag in the conversation to suggest to Jim that they bed down in anticipation of the journey the next day. Without giving Jim a chance to demur, he turned to Jeff and asked if they could bed down in the clearing on the grass. Jeff readily assented to that.

At that point Millie broke in saying that Jasper had said they were light on supplies and suggesting that she pack some to send along with them. To this, Jeff also cheerfully assented, refusing the offer of payment. He complimented Jim on his stories and jokes, saying that they'd been more entertained tonight than any supplies that they might send along would be worth.

Jim acted none to happy to be dragged away from the fire and the fun, but even he had to acknowledge that everyone here was tired. They bedded down on the grass a short way from the tents and within minutes, the only thing to be heard was loud snores.

Jasper woke the next morning to the first gray of dawn. quietly shaking Jim out, which was accomplished only with difficulty. They were on the trail before anyone in the camp had shown signs of life. This was according to Jaspers plan. Although he liked each and everyone there, he knew that if they stayed for breakfast, they'd be slowed at least a couple of hours. This he was unwilling to allow.

Jim was plenty grumpy as he led out. He cut across country for about three quarters of a mile before picking up the trail heading east. "It be a steep climb rat up heah 'bout near a mile. Gonna strain us bad 'thout we git us some nourishment." Jim grumbled.

"Well, le's get up the trail a bit, an' we'll stop an' see what Millie give us."

Jims answering grumble might have been a bit more cheerful, but the only thing that Jasper really heard was a "Hongry."

Jim hadn't been lying about a steep trail. It went up at a steep angle and it kept going up. It was probably three or four miles before they even came to a place level enough to stop and rest. For the whole way, Jim had been grumbling. Jasper had stayed about ten feet back and all he could discern of what must have been a considerable tirade was an occassional "Hongry."

When they stopped at the level place and sat down, Jim was most uncharacteristically silent. Jasper knew that this meant that Jim was some put out with the whole situation. He was surprised to see that Millie had put in the remains of the large trout from last night. It had weighed about four pounds and at least half of it remained.

In spite of himself, Jim brightened when he saw it. Two minutes after he began eating, he was mostly himself again. He began to tell a story of a place up ahead where he'd spent some time panning for gold. Jasper had refrained from asking questions until Jim got in a better mood, and he figured that had now happened. "How far do we gotta go to get to Glacier Creek, Jim?"

"Wal, it be a fer piece, friend Jasper. It be hard doin's an' long goin's." He shook his head.

Alarmed, Jasper asked, "What you mean hard an' long? How far is it?"

Jim inclined his head to look up the trail. He ruminated and scratched his beard. finally, "Ah 'spect it be ta most part a twenny, mebbe twenny fi' mile."

Jasper stared at him. "Twenny...Uh, twenty miles? Why that ain' such a ways. We can pro'bly be there early this afternoon."

Jim shook his head as he sadly regarded Jasper. "It be hard goin' friend Jasper. Hard doin's. Rat steep, it be. Rat steep an rough lak yu most nevah see."

Jasper looked up the trail, and then down. It had been steep so far. Hard going any way you looked at it, but as far as he could see, the trail seemed to be the same. He scratched his head, maybe Jim was just fooling him. Jims stories all seemed to be concerned with hard times of one kind or another, most so improbable that Jasper wondered if most weren't just made up to entertain people. Anyway, there was nothing to do but move on out. What ever was up there had to be crossed and the sooner the better.

Chapter Thirteen

Ten minutes after starting, Jasper began to get an idea to what it was that Jim had been trying to tell him. Minutes after starting from the place that they'd rested, they'd come to a fork in the trail. The trail that they'd been on, while steep and rough in places, was at least somewhat maintained. Logs that had fallen had been mostly cut and pushed off the trail. The very bad washouts had been at least somewhat filled in with dirt and rocks to provide footing on those difficult places. That trail continued off to the left. Jim took a dim trace that curved to the right.

Jasper followed with no more than a glance at the more attractive trail they'd just left. When they were stopped within fifty yards by a blowdown tangle that blocked their way entirely, he questioned it. Jim responded with a shrug, "This yere be ta way ta Glacier Crick." He said. "Ta othah way be ta Sinkin' Lake. Ah rutha be a goin' ta Sinkin' Lake, but thet don' be whut yu a wantin', be it?"

It had been exasperation with hitting hard going so soon that had made Jasper even ask the question of how come they had left the obviously better trail. He'd known that Jim hadn't taken this way for purely silly reasons. It was discouraging though. They had to buck their way into the thick brush around the blowdown. It took enough time that Jasper knew if they hit a lot of the same thing, it would be all of the slow going predicted by Jim when he'd asked about it.

The going didn't improve much for the next mile. They repeatedly were forced to detour around blowdowns. The only consolation was that Jasper found horse tracks in several places. These, he hoped and believed were the tracks of the rangers. He even convinced himself that he recognized Genevieves tracks, although he knew in his logical mind that he wouldn't actually know them from any other horses tracks that he might come across.

About a mile along, the trail left the canyon bottom and slanted steeply up the left mountain slope. Jasper was relieved to be out of the thick foliage in the bottom. That relief lasted for about five minutes. It took no longer than that for the steep slope that was filled with loose shifting rock to play him out so that he gaspingly begged Jim for a rest stop.

Jim pretended to be put out at the stop but the effect was somewhat spoiled by the panting gasps that puntuated his chiding of Jasper.

When Jasper could talk again, he asked, "How far does this keep up this steep?"

"Why, friend Jasper, this yere be jus' ta fust leetle bit a it." He took a long look up the slope. "Ah 'spect we gots ta mos' a seven, shoot, mebbe eight er nine mile afore we top out ta Sunshine pass." He took another moment to ruminate here. "It be sev'ral yeahs since ah be up this yere way but ah do b'lieve thet pass is bout neah more'n thu'teen thousan' feets up. An hard doings, it all do be." He finished sadly.

The heights that Jim had just sadly articulated meant less than they might have to Jasper since he really had no close idea of what the elevation was at their present location. Looking down the few hundred feet that was all they'd come since beginning to climb this switchback trail from the bottom made the seven to nine miles sound very bad indeed though.

Jaspers misgivings turned to be only too well founded. The day turned into a nightmare of going until they could go no more before taking rests that grew steadily longer as the day wore on. While most of the trail was simply very steep, they hit several slide areas where the trail was tenuous to say the least. In several places, the trail had disappeared entirely due to slide action. These areas were extremely dangerous to detour around due to the loose and treacherous nature of the surrounding slide rock. Jasper found himself wondering how in the world the rangers had used this trail with the horses. He frequently found hiself berating the rangers for bringing Genevieve along here and so putting her in jeopardy. That they had come this way was now frequently betrayed by tracks in the sheltered places they came to. This, indeed was the one bright spot for Jasper. He knew, or at least he believed that these were the rangers tracks. That kept his spirits up a little.

By this middle of the day, Jim was giving forth a nearly unbroken stream of grumbling. Jasper was just too worn out to pay any real attention to him. When they took a comparatively lengthy noon break to eat and try to ease the cramps from their muscles, Jim made up for the loss of wind while climbing that prevented him from voicing his grievances very loudly. That Jasper was just too tired to give him due attention, just seemed to make him more aggravated. Since he'd enthusiastically volunteered for this expedition, he couldn't very well fuss at Jasper. That was alright because he had other convenient targets, namely the rangers.

He pontificated long and hard about how they took the most aggravating places to go. That, he declared, they'd done just to spite him because of his mountain man penchant. They'd climbed right up this terrible mountain, and then down the equally terrible other side just to get back at him.

While Jasper had been paying little attention to the ranting, something seemed to cut through. He looked at Jim with shock, "What do you mean bout we gotta go down the other side a this mountain? An what bout it bein' jus' as bad as this here side?"

It took a few seconds for Jim to shift gears from persecution of himself by the rangers to Jaspers question. When he did, he shrugged, "Wal, we come up din' we? Er leastways, we be acomin' up." He regarded the still continuing slope disgustedly. "When we be a gittin to ta top, wal we gotta go down. It be jus' bout near as fer as comin' up."

"Well, but that's goin' down, now ain' it? Be more easier than this here goin' up, now won't it?"

Jim appeared to give this more than casual consideration before slowly answering. "Wal, in some ways, it be easier. Harder to control yore way though. Slip an slide a bunch more. Ya gotta be on guard more an thets tirin'." He shook his head. "They jus' ain' no way round it. Goin' down be jus' more dangerous than comin' up."

Jasper could find nothing encouraging at all in the answer. He dejectedly subsided into a rather morose silence for the remainder of the rest stop.

As they started up the trail again, both uttered many long and loud groans. They found however that the rest had done them good. It seemed that they'd gained something of a second wind and as long as they attacked the slope deliberately, the interval between rest stops lengthened.

It was less than an hour before sundown when they finally topped out on the narrow mountain ridge that dipped no more than slightly to form `Sunshine Pass'. The terrain up here was far above timber line and there was nothing more than low scrubby bushes and not many of them. There was however, thick and lush grass. They took advantage of the first level place on top to slump to the ground.

The second wind that they'd felt on leaving their noon rest had slowly disappeared to be replaced by nothing but raw nerve. Jim shrugged his arms free of the pack straps and laying down, used the pack for a pillow. His exhaustion was testified to by his complete disinclination to talk. As a matter of fact, it took only a couple of minutes for him to go to sleep as was testified by deep even breathing.

Jasper had slumped to the ground himself but although he was probably as exhausted as Jim seemed to be, he wasn't sleepy. After a short rest, he shrugged out of his own pack straps and climbing to his feet, he wearily moved across the couple of hundred feet of relatively level ground to where the trail plunged over into the far mountain canyon. He wasn't sure of what he'd expected. When they'd started up the trail this morning, he guessed that he'd had some idea that when they got up here, he'd be able to see something. Maybe even see Genevieve staked out on a meadow down there somewhere.

This canyon right where he stood was maybe five or six miles straight across to the top of the next ridge. There were places where it appeared to be even wider although it did narrow in places. The discouraging thing was that he could see several miles down the canyon before it made a sharp enough turn that the bottom could not be seen at all. Looking up it, he knew that he could see even further. Not only that but although the canyon turned, denying him sight of the bottom, he could see that it stretched several more miles. Although the sun still shown where he stood, the canyon itself was in deep gloom. He believed it to be somewhat less deep than the one they'd just climbed out of but it was plenty deep for all that. He could see the trail switchback steeply down just as Jim had said it would. He turned and dejectedly returned to the campsite.

Digging down deep in his pack for whatever available food, he brought to light the remains of the fish. There was very little left and he put it aside for Jim, settling for a cold can of beans. He'd looked around for something to burn and heat the beans up but the few anemic bushes that grew here left very few dead remains. He might have tried to gather some if he hadn't been so tired. As it was, he ate the beans without really tasting them. He made a weak try at waking Jim to eat. Jim just rolled over muttering before beginning to snore again. Jasper lay down and looked appreciatively at the bright sunset. This lasted for somewhat less than a minute when his eyes involuntarily closed and he slept.

Jasper woke as usual in the dim light before sunup. He opened his eyes to see, several miles away, a high mountain peak that had just caught the sun. The sun lit up a couple of hundred feet of the peak and the misty light fog hid the base of the mountain and made it seem that the glowing peak floated unsupported high in the air. It was such a novel sight that he lay silently and just looked. So engrossed was he that it was only gradually that he came aware of a strange sound behind him. When it finally got through, he jerked around. Jim was sitting eating something out of a can and when

Jasper jumped up, he ceased chewing for a moment to look at him curiously. "Som'pin wrong, neighbor Jasper?"

The sight of the hairy Jim stolidly spooning food out of a can was suddenly uproariously funny to Jasper. He erupted into laughter. Jim joined in to chuckle weakly a couple of times but he couldn't see anything funny and shrugging went back to his can of food and ignored Jasper. Deprived of an audience, he rapidly sobered. The laughter did him good though. He felt much better mentally as he climbed from his sleeping bag although the aches and pains of the extraordinary effort of yesterday made him groan piteously a couple of times.

"Whut be it yu want fer breakfast?" Jim asked, gesturing at a row of four cans lined up on a nearby flat rock.

Jasper frowned. "Is that all the food we got left?"

"Thet be 'bout it. Ah eat alla thet fis'. Warn't much lef' ennyhow."

Jasper shrugged that off. "Yeah. I know there wasn't much. I sure thought we had more cans a stuff though." Jim paid no attention, except to the can in his hand. After a short consideration, Jasper sighed. "Well, we better be payin' attention to gatherin' some roots or somethin' as we go along today. Them there won't last us long."

Jim seemed to have regained much of his good humor this morning. He must have slept well. Now he raised a negligent hand. "Jes' keep yu eye open fer game. Ah gots muh ol rifle loaded and ah be ready fer em." After a moment, he added, "Jes don' pint me at 'nother eagle though."

Jasper got up and stretched. "I think I'll save that food for later. I'm anxious to get on down that trail. I do believe you're right 'bout that down trail. It don't look noways easy."

Jim finished the can and tossed it over his shoulder. He scoopped the other cans into his pack and slipped it on as he climbed to his feet. "Wal, it ain' gone git a bit easier with us jes' a sittin' heah. Le's be gittin' down it." He moved out.

The trail proved to be every bit as treacherous as Jim had predicted. But there was just no doubt that going down as much easier physically than coming up had been. After a couple of slips that could have turned into something serious if they hadn't been on their guard, they set a slow enough pace that they were able to evaluate chancy places and formulate ways to avoid most of them. It was still a slow and exhausting process but not nearly as taxing as yesterday.

It was midafternoon when they finally turned the last switchback and the trail leveled out in the narrow bottom alongside the samll river. They'd exhausted the canteen long ago and nothing had ever tasted better than the icy water of the stream. They spent some time there before moving on. The tracks of the horses were clear to be seen heading up the canyon. Although it was two or three hours before real dark, the sun was already hidden by the mountain ridge they'd just descended. It was clear that darkness would fall early down here and Jasper was in a fever to get close to the rangers before that event transpired.

It was not to be. They traveled until it was simply impossible to discern tracks. Although they were exhausted, they'd kept up a good pace and Jasper figured they'd covered ten miles, maybe a bit more. The trail had been easy, following the bottom fairly faithfully, crossing the river when necessary to take advantage of all the flat going that was available. The trail was little used up here, more by the deer and elk that the rangers had come to count than by man. as a consequence, it was little more than a trace in most places. In some rocky places, it simply disappeared. It was easy to pick up again though in the narrow canyon bottom. It was obviously just too hard to get here for many campers or fishermen.

Jasper stopped and turned to Jim. "If we just keep goin' up here, we can't very well lose the trail, can we?"

Jim had kept his usual good humor all day, and it was intact now. "Wal." He opined, rubbing his nose and tipping his head to inspect the sky as if the answer was to be had there. "Ah don' thank we cud lose it if'n it keeps agoin' rat up this heah canyon."

Tired though Jasper was, he caught the nuance of that. "Yeah, I guess what you're sayin' is that they might turn off into one a these here side canyons, That it?"

"Rat as rain. Rat as rain, neighbor Jasper. Then thar ranger mens cud turn off heah er thar er ennywheah. Thar be no knowing as to whar them thar fellers be a goin' exact, 'cept it be round 'bout heah som'ers."

"This here canyon can't keep going forever. Don't ya think we gotta be gettin' close to em?"

"Wal, ta way ah 'member it is thet this leetle crick heads up on ta no'th side of a big ol' mountain in a leetle canyon thet don' git much sun. Not even in the summer. They is a snow pack thar what feeds it. It ain' a proper glacier, leastways ah don' think it be, but it be prob'ly ta nearest thang they is round 'bout heah. Thet be why they named it like they did though. Thang is, thets gotta be ten, mebbe fifteen mile more. They could be ennywhar 'long it. An then, they could take off in enny one of a bunch a side canyons 'twixt heah an' thar." He sighed. "Ah know thet yu a frothin' ta git on an' git yore hoss back. Ah gotta say though, friend Jasper, we cud lose thet trail entire if'n we goes on a fumblin' in ta dark."

Jasper quietly considered the options. He hated to admit it but the only thing that made any sense at all was to stop for the night and pick up the trail in the morning. Sighing, he stripped off his pack and and carrying it in his hand, moved off the trail in the direction of the stream, which here was forty or fifty feet west.

The camp was set up quickly, mostly because they were tired and all they did was start a small fire and unroll their sleeping bags. They'd found a few roots and plants today, eating most of what they found where they found them. They'd seen nothing that Jim could shoot though, and when they opened one can of the remaining food apiece, that left only that many more for the future.

Chapter Fourteen

They'd gone no more than a mile the next morning before coming to the camp site of the rangers. Although it would be some time before the sun shown directly on the small meadow in front of them, it was plenty bright enough to see the piles of horse droppings that dotted the grassy clearing.

Something told Jasper without going closer that he was too late. Maybe it was the look of the droppings that lacked the color that fresh droppings had. Shaking his head, he moved up to the meadow and began to move cautiously around the edge. He wasn't completely sure that the rangers had gone. They might have just moved the horses somewhere else. As he moved around though, he was able to tell that some of the droppings weren't all that old. He wasn't anything like an expert at diognosing the freshness of horse droppings but he'd have bet that some of what he was looking at were no more than a day old.

This was pretty much confirmed when about half way around, he came on the former campsite of the rangers themselves. The fire was cold and had been out for a long time, the ashes weren't blown around. This might have been less than a professional way to tell how long the fire had been out but Jasper felt that he was right.

Jim startled him when from behind, he cut into Jaspers reverie. "Yistady."

"What?" Deep into his own thoughts, Jasper didn't catch the others thought.

Jim gave him a level stare. "Yistady. Them thar ranger mens ain' been heah'bouts since yistady." He went to one knee to examine the sign more closely before opining. "Ah 'spect they pro'ly lef 'bout early mo'nin' yistady. Ah be thankin' long 'bout early mo'nin." He looked at Jasper and nodded his big head affirmatively.

Jasper moved over and leaned against a tree. "Dog--gone it. Ain't I ever gonna be able to come up with them fellers? Seems like the more we hurry, the worse we do."

There was sympathy in Jims eyes as he looked at Jasper and said, "Wal, friend Jasper, Jes' sit rat thar. Ah be agoin' an fandin' whichaway thet they went." He moved off across the clearing toward the trail.

Jasper slid down the tree until he was sitting and leaning back against the trunk. He was feeling definitely puny. The last couple of days of climbing and then descending the mountain had him feeling tired in spite of a fair nights sleep. Now he was feeling dejected too. It was at times like this that he had the urge to just quit and go back to civilation and do....what? That was the thing. What could he do if he was to go back? Make a fool of himself like he'd done before? And what about Genevieve? He wasn't sure that she'd been really mistreated by her former owners, but her skinny condition told him that she hadn't been adequately fed, if nothing else. He levered himself erect to await the return of Jim. No, there was nothing to do except keep after the rangers until he got Genevieve back. Nothing else would ever satisfy him.

Jim hollered from clear across the clearing, "This heah be the way them ranger mens went alrat. They tracks is justa agoin'. Come on."

Jasper lost no time in crossing the clearing to join him. Following to the trail that was on the far side of the thin brush of the clearing edge, he squatted and inspected the tracks. Although he'd come to have less than total confidence in Jims tracking abilities, the sign here in the trail was clear and unequivocal.

He stood and faced Jim. "This here's the trail to Jacks Creek then, huh?"

For a moment Jim appeared to be baffled. "Wal no." He said slowly as he thought about it. "Wal, this do be one a ta ways, but it be a bunch longer than 'tother way."

Alarmed, Jasper hurried to ask, "What do ya mean, this ain' the way. Jacks Creek is where they said they was goin', now ain' it?"

"Wal yeah. Jacks Creek be it. Ah'd jes fergot, is all."

"Well, tell me what ya mean 'bout this not being the best way to Jacks Creek. What are ya talkin' 'bout?"

"Now don go gittin' yuse'f in a uproar. It jus' do be thet if'n they went this way, they gone have to go 'bout near twice as fer. Ta way we come over ta mount'in is ta closest way."

"You mean Jacks Creek is back the way we come?"

"Wal, not 'xactly. 'Member thet Sinkin' Lake ah said 'bout when we started climbin' ta pass over thar? Wal, fum whar we tunned off up thet pass trail, it do be 'bout ten miles to ta lake fum thar. 'Bout near ten, mebbe twelve miles fu'ther is Jacks Creek." He turned and spent a few seconds contemplating the trail that paralelled the small river as far they could see it. Turning back, he informed Jasper, "Ah really ain' too sure a how fer them ranger mens'll have to go this way. Ah know this trail leads clear off down through the foothills rat to ta edge a ta wilderness area. Thet be mos' part a sixty er seventy mile, ah 'spect. It be jes 'bout near thet fer thet a trail takes off an' crosses a low pass inta Sinnets Creek. "Bout twenny mile up Sinnets Creek, Jacks creek comes in f'um ta southeast. Ah ain' ben over all a it ma-ownse'f, but ah be hearin' bout it fum this un and that un. Ah bet it be a hunnert, mebbe a hunnert an' fity mile." He shook his big head gloomily.

Jaspers mouth was hanging open. "Why in the world would they go that distance if they could go back over the mountain an' it's that much shorter?"

"Wal, ah were su'prised when they come over ta mount'in ta way they did. Thet's passin' bad goin' fer hosses. It mebbe thet they jes decided thet goin' the longer way was safer." He shrugged. "An' it also mount be thet they decided not to go to Jacks Creek ennyhow. Mount be they is headin' out a ta wilderness area altogether."

Jasper shook his head in exasperation. It seemed that each and every situation that they found themselves in turned into a question mark. He'd come into the wilderness to try to get away from complex situations. It had turned out to be anything but simple though. Now, what to do about this? If he could be sure that they were headed for Jacks Creek, it was clear that the thing to do would be to go back over the pass and so pick up valuable time. But if they were indeed headed out of the wilderness, then he needed to stick right on their trail and find where they went so he could follow them in the more complex world of civilaztion. He had surprised himself when he thought that last thought, but he realized that it was true. He'd follow where ever he thought it necessary to get Genevieve back. It had become a kind of Holy Grail search for him. If he failed, he'd be worth nothing to himself or anyone else. With that realization, he felt better, or at least more sure of his purpose.

"Well, we jus' gotta follow along, that's all. Right down the trail. And it looks like we better hurry if they left yesterday."

Jim looked a bit askance at that. He looked tired too and Jasper wasn't at all sure just how much he'd be able to hurry. Jasper was nothing if not determined though and right now, he was moving up the trail even as he swung the pack to his shoulders. He looked back to check just as Jim sighing moved along after him. Jasper knew he was as interested and committed to this as he was. He'd stick it out and follow along to whatever end this had. He, like Jasper, was caught up in it. There was no way he could stand to not be a part of whatever happened here. Jasper even heard him hum a little tune that was barely audible as he hurried along.

About noon Jim got a shot at a rabbit and connected. Both were hungry and they stopped right then and roasted it over a quickly kindled fire. Feeling stronger, they made better time for the first miles after. Coming on three grouse in a tree, they had their supper.

Their good luck seemed to last as they came on more rabbits and a couple of more grouse. With this going for them, they made good time and about midmorning two days after taking the rangers trail, they came in sight of the mens campsite on Jacks Creek.

The camp was in a nice grassy meadow off to the side of the Creek. They'd come close to the meadow before seeing the horses, which was the thing that told them they'd arrived.

Dropping into the brush, they waited motionless to see if an alarm was raised. They'd attracted the notice of one of the horses that had been staked out close to the side on some of the better grass.

Finally, hearing nothing, they cautiously moved close enough to see through the thinning brush. Sleeping bags hung over a low brush, along with pots and pans sitting by what must have been the fire site, marked the spot that they'd chosen to sleep and cook.

A further ten minutes of watching without seeing or hearing anything other than the sleepy movements of the horses convinced them that the rangers were absent.

The horse that had first noticed them, was simply standing and looking. The other animals that were further away were paying no attention. It took some neck stretching for Jasper to even see Genevieve. She was laying down on the far side of the meadow close to the camp site. The other two horses were lazily feeding close to where she lay. None were tied except the one closest that they'd alerted. That one must be the only one that was liable to stray, or else the rangers had figured that if one was tied, the rest would stick close and not leave it.

Jim turned and in a falsetto whisper, asked, "Yu agoin' in an git her rat now?"

Jasper had been contemplating that very thing but she was a full two hundred yards away over totally clear meadow that would provide absolutely no cover. Nonetheless, he was virtually ready to get up and move out to her, when the breeze carried the faint sound of voices. "Where's that comin' from?" He whispered sibilantly. He raised himself fractionally while his head swiveled frantically, trying to pinpoint the source without exposing himself.

"Ah ain' shore. Ah thank it be comin' fum thar." He pointed to a small side canyon that took off to the east just past the other mens campsite.

That advise turned out to be superfluous, because at that instant, both men came into sight only a hundred feet the other side of their camp. It appeared that they'd indeed been up the canyon that Jim had indicated. They must have been on a trail because they were making good time and they were clearly headed right for their campsite.

"Let's git outta here." Jasper hissed as he dropped low and squirmed backward. They quickly gained the thicker brush and were able to straighten to a crouch, with which they made much better speed.

A half mile down, they crossed the trail where thick growth grew right to the creeks edge. After slaking their considerable thirst caused by crawling around in the dust, Jim glumly asked, "Wal, yu got enny idees how yu gone go 'bout gitting yore hoss? Them thar ranger mens is liable to come up on yu when yu don' least 'spect it."

Jasper was thinking about it and feeling as glum as Jim had sounded. He finally shook his head as he advised, "Jim, why'nt you take a nap or something? I gotta figure something to do, but I ain't got no idea what yet."

Jim had already lain down and closed his eyes and so needed to do little to comply with that suggestion. He murmurred something that was lost to Jasper in his preoccupation, but it didn't really matter.

It was a good hour later to the accompaniment of Jims snores that the idea seemed to filter in. To go in and get Geneveive safely, the postion of the rangers would have to be fairly predictable. It finally came to him that the only times that the rangers were in the same place at the same time was at night. At night and in the early morning and late evening. After thinking that over, he came to the conclusion that the logical time would be evening. Night time would be complicated by not being able to find his way through the brush quietly. If he made much noise at all, even if it was not enough to directly alert the rangers, it would startle the horses and so alert the rangers in that way. He considered the morning seriously, as the time when the men would be least alert. After thinking heavily along those lines, he rejected that idea. He needed the help of Jim, and Jim was at his totally least alert in the early morning. His level of morning alert would make the rangers seem hyperactive. No, it would have to be in the evening. And if it was to be evening, it would be just as well to make it this evening.

That decided, he let his mind drift and in no more than minutes, his snores harmonized with those of Jims.

He was awakened by Jim moving around. A quick glance at the sun showed that it was about midafternoon. They still had a good part of the last rabbit and a bit of the last grouse they'd cooked. Predictably, that was Jims target now.

Seeing how fast those leftovers were disappearing and being cognizant that this was all there was until they'd be able to get far enough away from the rangers to safely shoot without being heard, he quickly sat up and scooted over to Jim.

Jim handed over part of what remained without comment and for a while they sat and silently finished their meal. Sighing, Jim leaned back against a small bank of dirt and fixed Jasper with a jaundiced eye. "Yu figger ary thang 'bout gittin' yu hoss back, neighbor Jasper?"

Jasper contemplated the sky for a moment. It would be a couple, maybe three hours until dark and to implement his plan, they'd have to wait for dusk. Now, he looked at Jim and explained. They would both move down close to the meadow and about the time the sun dropped behind the western mountain, Jim would go around and come in from the other side of the camp. He would toll the rangers out that way and keep them busy until Jasper could catch Genevieve and lead her away. That would give them plenty of time overnight to get a lot of distance between the rangers and them. He doubted that they'd try to follow anyway, but if they did, They'd have a lot of miles to make up.

Jim scratched his head absently as he considered it. "Ah 'spose it mount work." Was his dubious comment.

"Why won't it? You said them rangers wasn't lookin' fer you." He regarded him suspiciously. "They ain' after you, are they?"

Jim looked confused. "Wal no, they ain' arter me. Whut fer wud they be arter me? Ah ain' done nothin'."

"Why can't you go and toll them away then? If they ain't after you that is?"

Jim had finally got the drift of what it was that Jasper was talking about. "Aw no. It ain' thet they is arter me. Ah wuz jesta thankin' whut were ah gone tell em to git em to come wif me and keep em thar."

"Oh." Jasper said. He was silent as he considered the problem. Finally, he suggested. "How about if you was to tell 'em that you'd seen a funny animal just out there a ways."

"A funny animal?"

Seeing that he might have confused him, Jasper hurried along. "I didn't mean ha, ha, funny. A strange animal is what I'm thinking. You know, a strange looking animal that you hadn't seen before."

"Strange?" Jim slowly answered, as he thought about it. Jasper anxiously watched him, but he relaxed as a light seemed to come into Jims eyes. "A funny animal. Why sho. Ah thank ah mounta seen one wif big teeth an' big horns. Allimigator scales too, ah'm a thankin'."

Jasper frowned. "You don' wanta overdo it. Them there rangers might git suspicious if'n you was to tell 'em somethin' too outlandish."

Jim was clearly into this now. he waved a negligent hand. "Jes yu leave it ta me, friend Jasper. Ah got it in muh mind now, an ah'll fool em good."

As usual, when Jim got specific about something that he was going to do to help him, Jasper was anything but easy in his mind. Jim always seemed to take things beyond the bounds that most people considered normal and proper. It was a worrisome thing. He settled down as best he could to wait the intervening few hours. A couple of times, he nearly drifted off to sleep, but each time he was interrupted by muttering and low chuckles as Jim schemed and planned his deception of the rangers. No, he was anything but easy in his mind.

He found that he'd finally drifted off to sleep when Jim shook him. "It be near 'bout time, ah'm a thankin', neighbor Jasper."

Jasper sat up quickly, thinking he might have overslept and not trusting Jim to know just the timing that he'd had in mind. He saw, however, that it was just about right. The sun was maybe ten or fifteen minutes from dropping below the western ridge. Rising, he advised Jim, "Might be you better leave that there rifle gun here to camp. Them there rangers might not take it kindly if they was to think you was a huntin' them elk that they been a countin'."

Jim waved a hand dismissively. "Ah tolt yu, them thar ol' boys knows me. If'n ah was ta come inta thar camp wifout muh ol' rifle, them boys'd know thet thangs wasn't jes as they shud be. Ah best take it."

"Well, I suppose you know best about that. You sure don' wanta do nothin' that'll make 'em suspicious." He finished dismissively, already busy in his mind with what his part of this adventure would be. "I gotta rub some dirt on me so's they won' be able to see me good." He suited action to thought, to the dubious looks of Jim who obviously thought he was already so dirty that anything he did along that line was just redundant. If that was his thought, Jasper decided that he'd have to grant that he had a point.

Glancing at the lowering sun, he advised, "We best get along. We gotta be ready to move in fore it gets too dark. That'd be as bad as too light. Least I think it would."

Their timing seemed to be pretty good. They had good light to move through the thick cover along the creek that had to be negotiated quietly. Early dusk had arrived as they came to where the trail skirted the meadow on the east.

They could see the glow of a fire where the rangers camp was. Jasper turned to Jim and whispered, "Well, you know what to do. Get on around there and I'll get set on the edge of the meadow so's I can get Genenvieve and get on outa here just as soon as you toll them boys away. I'll meet you back at the camp and we'll get on out of here. Put as much distance betwixt us by mornin' as we can."

Jims grin was so wide, his teeth shown white in the tangle of beard and mustache. It was very clear that he had built himself up to this and was anticipating an enjoyable time fooling the rangers. "Ah be thar, neighbor Jasper, yu bet. Why ah bet....." His sibilant whisper trailed off as he moved off down the creek in preparation of cutting back to come in from the far side of the camp.

When his small noises had died away, Jasper turned his attention to his own problem. It didn't really appear formidable. The camp was along the south edge of the meadow and on the edge of the small draw that came out of the little canyon that they'd been in when Jasper and Jim had first seen them today. Light scattered brush grew for some ten to fifteen feet out into the meadow. Jaspers task, therefore, was to move quietly about half way down the meadow and there to wait for the sound of Jim leading the rangers off to the south. At that time, Jasper would move into the meadow and using the small tent rope that he always carried in his pack, he'd throw a loop around the horses neck and lead her away.

It was simple and with the rangers apparently busy with the preparation of their supper meal, he anticipated no real problems. It worked that way too. The brush was just thick enough to give him cover without being unduly noisy. He was quickly to the position that he figured to be most advantageous to his plan. Then he waited.

The dusk deepened and although he told himself that Jim hadn't really had time to get there yet, he worried that the frequently irresponsible mountain man might have made a wrong turn somewhere.

When he finally heard Jims voice though and looked across the meadow, he was gratified to see that it was just about as it should be. There was still plenty of light to see the horses where they grazed on the far side of the clearing. He lay his head down on his arm and tried to project a thought Jims way. `Don't get tied up with a lot of talk. Get them out of there.' He hoped that Jim would get the message somehow.

This state of affairs continued for some one or two minutes. Although Jasper could decipher nothing that was said, he could tell that Jims talk dominated that time. Only for a second or two a couple of times did the rangers manage to break in and say something. Having a idea of what Jim would be telling them, Jasper thought that they were probably asking questions about the `animal'.

At this time the volume of the talk changed, indicating that they were moving. It took a moment for Jasper to realize that the volume of the talk was growing. What was Jim doing? Instead of tolling the rangers the other way, they were clearly moving toward Jasper. He stretched his neck to try to see them. The folly of that occured to him immediately. He had already rubbed dirt on his filthy clothes and exposed skin to further camoflage himself. If Jim and the rangers were coming anywhere close, his only chance to escape notice was to hunker down and become totally motionless. He lowered his face into the dirt and tried to become one with it.

His worst fears were realized as he began to be able to make out what Jim was saying. "......Rat up thar when ah seen 'im. Turble thing, it were. Big ol' tee'fs. Horns lak yu most nevah see.............."

This went on and on but Jasper was no longer listening to Jims words. He was only aware of the fact that the rapidly escalating volume of his talk told of his leading the rangers right to where Jasper lay trying to melt into the ground.

No matter how he tried, Jasper couldn't conceive of what had happened to make Jim lead them here. He lay with both arms to the side and his hands forward past his head in the position that he thought would flatten him for the least exposure.

He didn't believe it. Mentally, he was shaking his head and muttering `no, no' in his mind. It did no good. Jim came as straight for him as if he knew exactly where he lay and stopped just as one of his big feet plopped on Jaspers hand.

Jaspers eyes flew open. If his head hadn't been turned away from the others, it's likely that they'd have seen the whites of his eyes shining as he silently screamed a protest. His hand was in the dust, which provided a cushion of sorts, but it felt as if the bones were being slowly pulverized. It was only with a superhuman effort that he was able to control the squawk that rose in his throat.

Jim stood there in all his majesty, telling of a mythical monster that defied the imagination of anyone that might have heard it, especially that of the rangers.

He heard one of them ask, "You drunk, Jim?"

"Drunk? Why ah'll have yu know thet ah ain had nary a drank." He swung around, the better to vent his indignation on them. In doing so, he ground the hand even deeper into the dust.

In spite of himself, Jasper let out a small grunt. Luckily, none of them isolated the sound to the ground just at Jims feet. One of the rangers nervously asked, "What was that?"

Jim answered just a trifle uneasily, "Ah don' know. It sounded kinda funny. Whut yu reckon it coulda been?" He moved back a few feet toward the rangers, freeing Jaspers hand.

Jasper was just able to stifle the sigh of pleasure he felt at the release of the huge pressure on his hand. But it was now clear that Jim and the rangers were a bit spooked. One of them said, "I don't believe I like the sound a that. It's jest a bit dark to see things good. Maybe we better git back to the fire. You say that thing was real big, Jim?" He finished uneasily as he moved back.

Chapter Fifteen

With the departure of the men, Jasper lost no time slithering back through the brush until he gained the cover of the thicker brush along the creek. Here, he took a moment to soak his hand, which had swelled up some. After just a couple of minutes of this, he cradled the hand to ease it from bumps and made his way back down the creek to their camp.

Back at their camp, he simply waited. He didn't want to build a fire because of the possibility that the rangers might see the glow. He did soak his hand while he waited and by the time Jim came pushing through the bushes a good hour later, the hand was much better.

Jim had no more than gotten into earshot when Jasper inquired, "What went wrong?"

"Wrong?" Jim inquired vaguely looking around nearsightedly.

"Wrong?" Jasper inquired again. "Yeah. what went wrong?" He repeated, becoming just a bit shrill this time around.

"Wheah 'bouts be yo hoss, friend Jasper? You got 'er, din' ya?"

"My hoss?" Jaspers voice seemed a bit hoarse to him with the strain of holding his temper. "I didn't get no horse. You know why I didn't get no horse?" His tone had risen toward the last to alert Jim that something was amiss.

Becoming solicitous, Jim moved closer as he asked, "Somepin go wrong? Ah tolled 'em away good. Thought you'd git 'er. Whut wuz yo trouble?"

Although there was no possibility of seeing Jims eyes in the dark, Jasper moved closer and looked at him. "What do you mean you tolled em away. What you did was toll 'em right to where I was. Right to where I was an' then stomped on my hand." He held up the still smarting hand in accusation.

Jims voice was totally confused. "What wuz yu adoin' out ta othah side a ta camp. Yu wuz 'sposed to be ovah by ta meadow. Wheah ta hosses was. Ah cain' see how yu cuda got tunned aroun' so bad that yu got on ta wrong side a ta camp."

Jaspers voice had deserted him. As always, when Jim did or said something so fantastic as to be totally unbelievable, Jasper would have to stop and think for a minute or two to see if Jim was playing a joke. By now though, he was convinced that Jim just wasn't capable of this kind of jest. After no more than a short thought, he believed the situation to be exactly literally as Jim had said it. Somehow, someway, he'd became disoriented in the dusk and led the rangers exactly the wrong direction. Leading them along the edge of the meadow instead of the other way.

This wasn't really hard to accept when he thought just a bit. He'd known since he'd met Jim that he had trouble seeing in the dusk. He just hadn't thought about it when they'd made the plan. Well, if he accepted that, and he did, then there was absolutely no point in pursuing it any further. Jim hadn't done it on purpose at all.

With a deep sigh, he said, "Well, it's done. I didn't get her, but there's always next time." Another thought occured to him. "Did you say anything about the camp here?"

Jim gave a massive shrug. "They ast me whar muh camp wuz. Ah jus' tolt 'em it were down ta creek a piece."

With another sigh, Jasper said, "Well, we better move just in case they might come lookin' fer you."

Jim scratched his beard while he thought. "Ah reckon thet be sense. Whar at kin we move?" He added, swinging a small burlap bag from his shoulder where Jasper had failed to notice it, "Them thar rangers give me some canned goods. They said they be long on food an' this wouldn't run 'em short."

Although this was welcome news, Jaspers preoccupation with the events of the night prevented him from giving it much attention. He brought his attention back to the problem at hand. "Well, we better move away from the creek. I figure that's where they'd look if they was to come along. Maybe 'crost the creek. Looks to be purty good cover over that way."

It was only the work of seconds to pick up the few things they'd unpacked and repack them. they were quickly across the creek and in the thick cover over there. There was a sickle moon up that shed a silver light. It only seemed to have the effect of making it even more absolutely dark under the trees where they were trying to walk. The stumbled along for maybe a couple of hundred yards before giving up. Doing no more than rolling their bedrolls out, they turned in. The morning would be time enough to think about the next thing they'd try to do.

The next morning was anything but cheerful. During the night, the sky had clouded over and it was a misty sprinkle that awoke them. The grey cheerless sky and the slowly thickening rain convinced them that a fire would probably be a safe thing right now. If they kept it small, it was unlikely the smoke would be noticed and the cheer that a small blaze bring was necessary to buck them up.

Jim heated something from what the rangers had given him last night. It was welcome, but Jasper was deep into trying to come up with another plan and he couldn't have said what it was that he ate. He could come up with nothing that gave much confidence and finally, he asked Jim if he had an idea.

"Ah don' know, friend Jasper. Whyn't we jus' go 'long purty soon an see the lay a ta land. Mebbe we c'n git an idee then."

Jasper sighed. "I guess you might be right. I sure 'nough cain' come up with much of anything." He looked out into the gently falling rain. "There ain' much sense a thrashin' aroun' in that wet brush. Make a lot a noise an' git wet as if we was to go swimming. Le's jus' wait here 'til that rain lets up a bit."

Jim was agreeable to that and although the thick trees above them didn't shield them completely, there was no more than an occassional drop coming through. This didn't bother them unduly and they lay down and slept.

It was after noon that the rain let up enough to encourage their excursion. Even by judicious detouring and careful negotiation of tight places, by the time they regained the trail, they were wet from their waists down.

Jim looked down at his wet clinging buckskings pants and muddy boots disgustedly. "Friend Jasper, it do be tough travelin' in this yere rain. An if we gotta git down in it ta git outta sight, we gone be even wetter all over."

Jasper was feeling no more cheerful about all of this than was Jim. "Well, le's jus' go down enough to see what it is that they're a doin'. I ain' no more anxious to get down inta that wet brush than you are. If we stay fer enough away though, might be we can come up with an idea without gettin' ourse'vs any wetter'n we are."

Jim waved him up the trail without further comment. They'd just started when the sun came out. With things seeming more cheerful, they topped the small rise in the trail where they could see a piece of the meadow that the rangers camp was situated on. Jasper stopped and looked. Somthing was bothering him. He couldn't see any horses but since he could see only a small part of the meadow, that part didn't escpecially alarm him. It took a second to figure what it was. There was no smoke from a camp fire. Knowing how wet and miserable they'd got just coming the short way from their camp, it just didn't make sense that the rangers would be out in this. He guessed that it had been in his mind that he'd be able to see the smoke from their campfire as evidence of where they were. He stood wondering what the absence of the smoke meant.

Without bothering Jim with his doubts, he moved down the trail. More of the meadow came into view until they could see it all. No horses. Jasper turned to look at Jim. The big moutain man was pulling at his beard thoughtfully. He spoke first. "Whar yu reckon they hosses is at, neighbor Jasper?"

"It looks as though they ain' there no more, Jim." He considered. "Look, they won't think much of it if you go in there. If they're still there, that is. Why'nt you go on along an see what happened. If they've gone somewhere, try an' pick up their trail. See where they went."

Jim nodded his big head, "Ah'll do it friend Jasper. Them there ranger mens din' say a thang 'bout goin' ary whar." He finished accusingly.

Jasper nodded distractedly. "Well go see what there is to see. If they left, we gotta git on their trail."

Jasper moved back up the trail until he could see part of the meadow while still sticking to cover. It was no more than minutes that he saw Jim crossing the meadow. Shortly after that, he came back the same way he'd gone.

As Jim came up the trail toward Jasper, he was studying it closely. "Ah b'lieve them thar fellers came rat along heah. Do ya see it, friend Jasper?"

Jasper hadn't thought of looking at the trail. For one thing, he'd noticed that the rain had erased even their own tracks of yesterday. Now he turned his attention to it. There were definitely horse tracks there, but Jasper aknowledged that he could make nothing of what he was seeing. "Why, there ain' been nothin' over here since the rain." He was suddenly struck by a thought. "You don't think they left before the rain Jim, do ya?"

"Wal, eithah before or durin'. They ain' a track down thar be airy fresher than whut yu a seein'. They lef' las' nat, er early this yere mo'nin. Thet's whut ah'm a thankin'."

Jasper shook his head. This seemed to be too much. "If they didn't talk about leaving, why would they just up an' go? Did they say they was done with their elk countin?"

Jim was again stroking his beard thoughtfully. "No. Fac' is, they said they still had a couple a places to look. Ah been a thankin' neighbor Jasper, yu reckon ah coulda scart 'em off wif muh talk about thet thar tur'ble ani-mule."

In spite of the unlikelihood of this idea, Jasper gave it a moments consideration before deciding that it didn't matter anyway. If the rangers were gone, they were gone. "Where you reckon they went, Jim?"

"Ah reckon thet ta ony place they be lakly to go is back ta they headqua'ters. Ah din't thank they was goin' rat away, but ta reason they give me thet food is thet they was most done with what they was doin'." He added belatedly. "This yere trail'd take 'em out a ta wilderness. They is back roads thar thet they c'n use ta ride rat back to Laran. Thet's one a ta main district ranger haidqua'tas."

Jasper didn't question the accuracy of Jims theory. He did pause to wonder how the seemingly single minded and backward Jim knew so many of the details of the surrounding civilization that he supposedly had totally abandoned. The thought didn't survive the whirl of other thoughts that were literally making him dizzy right now.

He slumped to the ground. "Well, I guess that does it for me." His tone was sad and resigned.

"Aw naw. Naw, friend Jasper. Why we'll foller along an' go rat to thar haidqua'tas. That thars jus' whut we'll do."

For a moment, Jasper began to hope. Then, as he reviewed in his mind the obstacles that faced them in such an endeavor, his spirits plunged even further. "Jim, I do appreciate your help and your offer of more help. I don' think you know what we'd be facin' though." He paused while he gestured to Jim and then to himself. "Lookee at us. I look like a filthy ragpicker. Worse'n them even. An' how 'bout you? Don' git me wrong. You look fine to me, but think a how they'd look at you out in civilization." He snorted. "Pro'ly throw us both in the hoos-gow, er maybe the funny farm." He ended up by staring miserably at the ground.

"It ain' thet bad, friend Jasper. We git ourse'ves cleaned up an we can go rat along."

Jasper was growing a bit irritated that Jim just wouldn't face facts. "Jim, where we gone get cleaned up? We ain' got no money to rent us a room. Even if we did, they wouldn't rent a room to a couple a fellers that look as rough as we do. An then, you may know where the ranger headquarters is. But what about where it is that they keep the horses? How we gone find out where that is. We ain' got no kinda car to ride around in. First guy that see's us walkin' around is goin' to call the law." He shook his head again, "With no money an' no car, I reckon we ain' got no chance."

Jim couldn't contain himself, He jumped up and paced up and down. "But, friend Jasper, we got all them things. Ah got 'em, an plenty mo' fer us."

Jasper seemed to have hit a low bottom in his emotions. As strange as it seemed, he wasn't even really interested right now. He asked rather tonelessly. "What is it that you mean, Jim?"

"Ah got a house an' a car." He paused a moment. "Why, ah got fo' houses an' a bunch a cars. Wal cars an' pickups an trucks. We go rat along an' git ourse'fs cleaned up. Then we go rat along to ta ranger haidqua'tas an' see ta haid ranger. Ah know 'im an' he'll tell me 'bout yo hoss, yu bet."

In spite of himself, Jaspers interest was kindled. He had no idea of what Jim was talking about. It had to be some kind of delusion. Jim was good at tall tales, he knew that from first hand experience. What would be the reason for him telling some thing like this, though. It would be simple enough to disprove when they tried to do what he said. "Maybe you better explain how it is that you got all those things."

Jim shrugged. "Wal, they is on muh ranch. Er, on muh ranches. Ah gots four a 'em."

Jaspers eyes had narrowed and his attention was now total. "What do mean, ranches?"

Jim looked confused. "Ah mean muh ranches. Ah gots four ranches."

Jasper was now totally intrigued. "You mean you got four ranches? What is it that you're doin' up here then?" Something else occured to him then. Maybe Jim was talking about the urban term for ranches. Little things of fractional acrage. "How big is all these ranches, Jim?"

"Ta answer yo' fust ques'tin, ah thought ah tolt yuh why. Them thar comminists was a tellin' me what ever an' all ah cud do wif mah own land. Ah wudn' put up wif it. 'Bout ta second part, how big they be." Here he paused to consider. "Wal all tagether, ah reckon they is a bit more'n sixty five, maybe sixty six thousan' acres."

Jasper realized that his jaw was sagging. He moved closer and looked into Jims eyes. Exhaling slowly, he said, “Jim, I think you better tell me how you got all that acreage. Will you do that?”

Again Jim gave a massive shrug. “Why sho’ly, friend Jasper. If yu is inter’ested ah’ll be mo’ then glad to tell ‘bout it. My grandpa homesteaded ta fust part. co’se, it was jus’ a bit a land thet he got thet way. By ta time he died, he’d bought more’n twenty thousan’ mo’. My Dad wuz content ta jus’ ranch whut we had, but when ah took ovah, these othah places come on ta markit at such a low price thet ah bought ‘em, nevah been sorry eithah. Ah made a lotta money. Got a lotta money.”

“Jim, this isn’t just a story is it? You really got all that free and clear. Why what you talkin’ ‘bout must be worth millions?” His tone made the last part a question.

The shrug again. “Ah ‘spect it’s wuth a pile a money alrat. Ah gots money though. Ah don’ need none more.”

At this point, Jasper began to believe. He’d been around Jim long enough that he believed he knew when he was sincere. “Well, do you got cattle on ‘em? You got somebody runnin’ ‘em?”

“Lemme tell ya somepin. Ah had a big operation goin’. Mount a ben ta biggest in Sachez county. Ah were tolt one time that ah wuz payin’ bout half ta taxes thet were paid in ta whole county. Thangs were goin’ ‘long purty gud ‘til ah were gone built a leetle shed down close ta one a muh hay fields. Had it mostly built when ta environmental protection people came in and tolt me thet ah were builtin’ on a wetland area.” Here he paused to snort and think back on that time. “Thet place were ever bit a quartah, mebbe a haf mile fum airy water. Ah tolt ‘em whar ta go an’ chased ‘em on they way. Thu’ty minutes latah, they come back wif ta sh’rf an’ he arrested me. Now ah knew ta sh’rf. Friends, ah thought we was. C’os, ah know thet he were under a turr’ble pressure f’um those slimy leetle snakes a environmentalists. Comminists all, ah say. Ah still thought it were a joke when they took me to ta jedge. Ol’ jedge Peters. Wal, he knew it weren’t rat, but he cudn’t do nothin’ fer me. He were under ta same pressures. Fined me a thousan’ dollahs an’ a suspended Jail term thet wud come unsuspended if ah were ta built ennythang without ta slimy environmentalists approval." Remembering must have been too much for Jim. He sat looking at the ground and shaking his head sadly.

Jasper cleared his throat.

Jim took the hint. "Yeah ah know. Ah went on home an' thought 'bout it. Ah had a lot a money in ta bank. 'Nough to last me if all ah wanted wuz ta pay muh prop'ty taxes. Well, really more than 'nough to pay fer ennything ah were wantin' fum now on. Ah rounded up muh cattle an' give 'em to charity. Ah did thet so ah wudn' have ta pay no taxes ta them people on ta money ah'd have got if ah were to sell fer a profit. Ah clost all the places down. Now ta on'y fellers ah gots wukin' fer me is three thet ta on'y thangs they do is patrol ta propity lines lookin' fer gov'mint peeples tryin' to come aroun'. Oh yeah. Ah gots me a lawyer thet works full time puttin' suits on gov'mint agencies. An a 'ccountant thet spends alla his full time mekkin sure thet muh investments don't no more'n pay fer expenses. Thets so ah don' pay none income taxes."

He thought a moment before shrugging. "Ah guess thet's 'bout it. But ah do gots ta thangs thet'll hep us ta git on an fand yo' hoss. It be 'bout mebbe fity er sixty mile to one a ta line shacks on ta back side a one a muh ranches. Ah keeps a pickup thar. We go rat along, clean up jes' a leetle. Then we c'n go rat along ta big ranch house. We can git clothes an' ever' other thang thet we want thar. Ain' no reason we cain' go rat along after yo' hoss then."

Jasper sat looking at Jim stupidly. He had to try twice before he got it out, "No. It don' look like there's any reason at all."

Chapter Sixteen

To take the established trails to Jims line shack would have more than doubled the distance. Jim said they could beat their way across country and that turned out to be a fairly accurate description of what they did. Detouring around only the worst of the thickets and cliffs. Only occassionally letting some of the highest peaks turn them from the line they desired, it seemed to be him and Jim that ended up taking the beating.

What would be only a day, or a day and a half at the most on good trails, took them the best part of three full days. They were a sight when they finally stood in front of the small log cabin. It was a fairly substantial building. Jasper had read of line shacks and had in his mind that one would be little more than a place a cowboy would roll out his bedroll. this one had a kitchen and a fair sized bedroom that had a bed that looked so good and soft that it very nearly overpowered Jasper. With an effort, he moved back to the kitchen.

The only water available at the line shack was out of a hand pump from a shallow well out behind the cabin. It was so icy cold that washing was a miserable chore. Jim didn't really wash at all, saying that the main ranch house would have hot water.

After only thirty minutes at the cabin, Jim led the way to the pickup that sat to the side. In spite of being extremely dirty, it was a four wheel drive that was only a couple of years old. It must have been kept in good shape by someone because in spite of being here for four months, which was what Jim said, it turned over just a few times before roaring to life. There was still a couple of hours of the days sun when they left to go to Jims main ranch house.

This trip wasn't something that Jasper had looked forward to without qualms. He'd remembered the many times that Jim had seemed to be unable to see, or at least to seem to see poorly. He was pleasantly surprised to see now, that Jim seemed to drive quite well. He stared straight at the road as though he might not be seeing it as well as he might, but he kept to his own side and when they turned onto a paved highway that had moderate to heavy traffic, he handled it well. Jasper relaxed and watched the civilization that he'd been away from for a time.

The ranch house was, in spite of Jims talk of having all the money that he'd ever need, a revelation. Two stories high, it must have had twenty rooms. It was kept in good shape by someone, maybe by the same men that also guarded against government intruders.

There must have been at least an acre of grass in front and it had only recently been cut. The building was built of cut stone with white recently painted trim. It looked like anything but an empty house, but when Jasper asked about servants, Jim said there weren't any. He assuaged Jaspers curiousity about the well kept appearance by saying that it was indeed the men that guarded the land boundaries that did the upkeep when they had the time for it. They obviously had taken the time for it lately. The house and its setting was a real jewel.

The inside showed a bit more of the neglect that it obviously suffered. It was not entirely forgotten, but the men must be much better outside than in. Here and there, dust could be seen. The vacuuming had not been done enthusiastically in tight places and corners. It was only because he was kind of expecting the inside to match the care of the outside that he saw it. Jasper was not at all particular. Once he'd noticed these things, he promptly forgot them. Jim sheparded him upstairs and showed him to a room with its own bathroom. "Whut size clothes yu wear, Jasper? Muh own clothes sho won' fit ya. Ah'll call an' git somepin sent in."

Jasper closed the door no longer doubting that Jim would be able to do those kind of things. The first thing he did was draw a hot bath and sink down into the suds.

He was in a fever to get on about the business of finding and somehow recovering Genevieve but when a half an hour later, he crawled from the bath and took a moment to lay down on the bed, he was asleep in a second. Jim, looking in a little later, smiled and left him to his rest.

The first thing Jasper saw the next morning when he opened his eyes was a pile of clothes stacked on a nearby chair. It took a moment to recover his wits enough to remember where he was, so deep had he slept. Turning over, he spied a clock on a bedside table that registered eight forty eight. He frowned. It had been evening when he lay down and right now he felt much more rested than an hour or two of sleep should have benefited him. Only then did the possibility come, that it might be morning instead of evening. No hint of light came through the thick curtains. He thought it possible that the reason there wasn't any light coming through them was because it might be the dark of early evening. When he pulled the heavy curtains aside, bright sunlight streamed in and he knew that his fears were realized. It was morning and he'd lost the chance to go after Genevieve in the dark of night.

Totally disgusted with himself, he indiscriminately grabbed a pair of pants and a shirt from the pile. Throwing them on, he briefly regarded the two new pair of boots, finally picking his own worn ones to wear because of the comfort. As he was heading for the door, he got a look at himself in the mirror and so surprised himself that he stopped and just stared. Of course, he knew that he'd grown a beard but it had been so long since he'd seen himself in a mirror that he'd simply forgotten. He remembered himself from when he'd been clean shaven, or at the most with a few days growth of beard. The stranger that stared back at him from the mirror had a beard that four or five inches long.

He shook his head, aggravated at himself for thinking such things when he should have been out trying to get Genevieve back, should have been out getting her back last night.

He had no idea of what room Jim might be in and so just went on downstairs, walking lightly as though there might be someone here that would think he was an intruder. He found an enormous living room with most of the furniture covered. The next room was a dining room with a table big enough to seat twenty or thirty people. It might have just been his association with Jim but Jasper got the idea that it had been a long time since this room had been used. The next room was the kitchen and although it was as deserted as the rest, he looked no further.

Rummaging in the cupboards and shelves, he found coffee and got it on the electric cook stove. Looking further while it brewed, he found the double wide refrigerator to be well stocked. Surely they didn't keep it like that all the time. Most of the stuff that he could see was dated material. They'd have to clean it out on a regular periodic basis. He decided that it must have been stocked last night. Jim wasn't the kind to require the princely treatment of having to have it stocked on a permanent basis.

Soon, the smell of bacon and eggs joined that of the perking coffee. He'd have bet those twin smells would root Jim out, and he'd have won. It wasn't quite ready when Jim pushed his way through the door.

"It do be a fan mo'nin', don' it friend Jasper?"

Jasper took a moment to stare at his friend. He'd discarded the buckskin suit alright and he was dressed in modern western clothes. He had on a suit that must have used quite a number of yards of electric blue cloth. The gleam of polished leather came from his boots. A gleaming white shirt with a western style bolo tie completed his atire. In its way, it was nearly as garish as the buckskin had been. Somehow though, Jim, in spite of his bushy uncut hair and thick beard, made it look stylish and easy, with none of the ludicrous look that someone with less presence would have projected.

Now he gave a fatalistic shrug. "I shoulda been out huntin' for Genevieve 'steada sleepin' like a hog in clover all night." He said a bit glumly.

"Wal, yu sho' 'nough needed yu sleep, ah'm a thanking. Ennyhow, they gots three er fo' places thet she cud be. We be bettah off ta jes' go long an talk ta ranger Long, down to ta haidqua'tahs."

Jasper had considered that when Jim had suggested much the same thing up in the mountains. He'd rejected it then and he reluctantly did so now. "Jim, we can't jus' go on in there an' ask 'bout a horse that we ain' even s'posed to know 'bout. We gotta figure something to say that won't make 'em suspicious."

Jim shrugged. "Ah's jus' agonna ast 'em 'bout a brown hoss thet strayed fum ta place heah. Ah gots a good ten mile a fence thet backs 'gainst ta f'rest service land. We usta have a man thet din't do nothin' cept chase strays up in ta f'rest land. We ain' got nothin' lef' 'cept ta leettle remuda fer ta boys thet rides fence, but we gets a stray ever now an' again even now. Ah thank thet me askin' 'bout a brown strayed hoss won' mek 'em 'spicious."

Jasper thought about that. It seemed to be a reasonable thing. "An' then they'll just take us along an' we can see what they got." Jasper beamed. But a follow up thought quickly sobered him. "Jim, I ain' exactly told things jus' like they happened." He briefly told the story of stealing the pickup and trailer, and of course Genevieve. "I didn't know how you'd take it an' I didn't want ya to think bad a me. But you can see that if we was to go in and pick her out now, an' they already know that she was the one stole like that, we'd be putting ourselves right where we don' wanta be."

Jim ponderously considered what he'd just heard while Jasper squirmed uncomfortably. If Jim decided that he wanted nothing to do with a horse thief, and Jasper had always read that westerners considered that to be a serious crime, he had no idea of what he'd do. He had began to depend on Jim so that the thought of not having him there for support was a definite dread now that he faced just that possibility.

So it was that Jasper was mightily relieved that when Jim finally spoke, it seemed that he'd only been considering the possible consequences, rather than any judgement of Jasper for what he'd done. "Ah guess thet mount be a roadblock ta jes' gittin' her when we see her all rat." Here a grin cracked the whiskers. "Ah were a wantin' ta do it sneaky ennyhow. Ah druther go long in thar an' git her ta night rat fum under they noses. Mek 'em squirm a leetle when they try ta explain whut it be thet happened."

Heartened by Jims attitude, Jasper asked, "But to do that, we gotta know where she is. What you reckon is the best way to do that?"

"Why, we go rat along jes' ta way we was gonna. Go rat ta rangah Long. Tell 'im ta same story. Ony thang, when we finds where she be, we jes' don' let on. Then we come back heah an' gits a hoss trailah. 'Pendin' on whar she be, we c'n mek a plan on how to go 'bout gittin' her."

Mightily relieved, Jasper lost no time in congratulating Jim. "I like it. Let's git on 'bout it, what d'ya say?" They'd finished eating while they talked and now they left the dishes for later in their hurry to implement the plan.

Jims driving had changed none at all overnight. He appeared to do a lot of squinting at the road and he drove just a bit fast for not seeming to see quite as good as he should. Overall though, he seemed to take safety seriously. Jasper relaxed and enjoyed looking at things.

It must have been no more than ten miles to ranger headquarters because even going through the moderate sized town of Laran, they were there in twenty minutes. The buildings were in a pretty setting with a good acre of grass in front that was a bit overdue for mowing. The thick grass was inviting though. There were also some of the prettiest small trees and bushes that Jasper had ever seen. As they approached closely, a sign on the building front announced that this was the `Headquarters, Hiute Forestry District.'

The ranger on duty at a desk in the office greeted Jim deferentially. He startled Jasper a bit when he refered to him as mister Fustz though. Jim rolled his eyes in Jaspers direction disgustedly and leaned close to whisper, "They jes won' 'cept thet ah'm a mountin' man heah."

Although the whisper was loud enough that it was for sure that the ranger heard, he paid no attention as he led the way down a short hall to an open door. As he ushered them inside, Jasper saw a plaque on the door proclaiming that this was the office of Theodore Long, Chief Ranger of the Hiute Forest District.

Ranger Long was a medium tall man who carried a bit of extra weight without seeming to be oversized. His hair was mostly gray, as was the bushy mustache he wore. He was dressed in the uniform of a forest ranger with bars on the collar that must have denoted his rank. He came around the desk with his hand extended. "Homer. How are ya doin'? Been a while since I seen ya. Are ya keepin' all right." He seemed to genuinely like the hairy mountain man.

For his part, Jim responded rather stiffly. Jasper figured that was because of the ranger using the discarded name. "Ah reckon ah been alrat." Courtesy forced him to ask, although rather tonelessly, "Yu doin' alrat, yu ownse'f?"

Ranger Long inclined his head. "Tolerable. Gettin' old, as you can see, but otherwise I'm gettin' along." He waved them to the chairs that were ranged along the front of the desk. "Have a seat." He moved back to his own upholstered chair behind the desk.

Without further invitation, Jim said. "This here's Jasper. We's acomin' ta see 'bout a hoss thet done strayed inta ta for'st land. Brown hoss, it be. Yu done found airy hoss thet looks lak that?"

Ranger Long looked bemused. He hesitated answering for a moment, as though puzzled. Finally, he said, "Ya know Homer, over the years, musta been a hundred of your strayed horses in the forest. Some we found. Most, you found your ownself. I never knew you to come and personally look for one of them though. Somethin' special 'bout this one?"

Jim looked startled. He obviously hadn't given any thought as to how this might look. It probably hadn't occured to him at all that looking for strayed horses was something that he'd always relegated to one of his men. He made a false start before hitting on anything to say to that. Finally, he said, "Wal, ta men be busy wif othah thangs rat now. Naw, it don' be thet they is airy thang special 'bout this heah hoss." Then he must have been inspired. "Yu know yo' ownse'f thet we ain' gots all too many hosses lef' now ennyhow. Cain' let airy a 'em git away."

This must have satisfied the ranger as he seemed to lose what small interest he'd had in the matter. "Yeah. I do know that you don't have near the horses that you used to. Darn shame too. Homer, I just can't understand why you're wasting time fooling around up in them mountains tryin' to be something you ain't."

This brought fire to Jims eye. “Now jes a minute. Yu knows whut.......”

This must have been a ongoing debate with them. Ranger Long forestalled any more of it with a weary gesture. “I know. I know.” He shrugged with a long sigh. “I don’t know what-all stock they’ve picked up lately. Most likely be over to Piney Meadows if they found it. If not there, it’ll have to be over to Jacobs Stable if we got it. The other place is closed down now. Budget restraints, ya know.”

Jim seemed to be a bit upset, probably at nearly being caught without a reasonable explanation for being here personally. He mumbled an inaudible reply as he got to his feet and headed for the door.

Jasper quickly tossed a “Glad I met ya” as he followed.

In the pickup, Jim gave a sideways glance. “Ah don’ thank we made ‘im much ‘spicious. Whut yu ‘spose, neighbor Jasper?”

“Naw, I think he jus’ thought it was kinda strange ‘til you told him ‘bout yore men bein’ busy. I don’ think he thought much of it after that.”

Jim sighed. “Ah hopes not. Ah nevah give no thought ‘bout whut thangs he mount ast me. Wal, we jes hope fer ta best, ah guess.”

“Aw, what could he suspicion anyhow? He don’t have no idea of who I am. I sure don’t think he seemed to suspect you of anything. Leastways, nothing but running around up in the mountains.”

Jim seemed to grimace under the beard. “Yeah. We wuz purty close friends once. He thinks ah shud a stayed an kep’ on.” The thought seemed to weary him and he shook it off. “Le’s git on an see ‘bout yu hoss, whut yu say?” Without giving Jasper a chance to reply, he started the pickup and pulled into the street.

“Ya know where this Piney Meadows is at?” Jasper asked.

“Ah knows ‘bout it alrat. Ah thank thet we jes check Jacobs Stable fust, though. Seems ta me thet be ta mos’ lakly place.”

Jasper figured that ranger Longs suggestion to check Piney Meadows first might just have something to do with Jims wanting to reverse the priorities of where to look. He left it alone though, with nothing more than a mental shrug.

Jacobs Stable proved to be about five miles into the country, back toward the mountains. It was a pretty place, all done up with white painted fences around the grassy riding meadows. The meadows were busy with young riders, some not so young too. It seemed that the Stables was a horse rental and riding academy.

Jasper looked nonplussed. "What would they be doin' with Genevieve here? This here looks like a private ridin' place."

"Thet jus' whut it be. Ta rangers brang some a ta hosses heah thet they wants ta keep away fum ta othahs fo' some reason er othah. Gots a contrac' wif 'em heah 'bout doin' it."

While Jim went to the office to see about any goverment horses that might be here, Jasper walked to the fence and leaned looking for his horse.

The meadow on the other side of the fence was about two or three acres in extent. There were probably a dozen riders meandering here and there, some being sheparded by others who gave advice loudly and with extravagant gestures. As far as he could tell, there wasn't a horse out there that could be Genevieve, although some were a fair distance away. The colors just weren't right.

He hadn't really expected to find her in this setting. If she was indeed here, it was likely that she'd be isolated somewhere away from the main business here. He still felt disappointment at not immediately seeing her though.

Jim came striding out of the office and called for him to come on. They rode for about a half a mile to a meadow that was hidden from the office and the main meadows by a thick stand of pine trees. There was a small stream rippling through the middle of this meadow and several horses grazed there.

At first glance, there was two that was possibilities. Something didn't seem just right to Jasper, but he felt hope rise in him anyway. There was no white painted wooden fence here, just stretched barbed wire. This gave him some trouble, but he eventually got over and hurried forward.

The horses had all been alerted to their presence by Jaspers antics in getting over the fence and were all staring their way with an alert heads up attitude.

His hurrying steps slowed as he realized that there was just nothing about the two possibles that was really familiar. He went on anyway to make sure, but stopped well back. There was absolutely nothing about them that resembled her up close. He turned and slowly and dejectedly walked back.

Jim had gotten the message and as Jasper came to the fence, he commisserated, "Wal, it warn' much lakly thet she'd be heah ennyhow. We fand 'er out ta Piney Meadows. Ah purty shore 'bout it now." Jasper didn't bother to point out that he'd chosen this place because of its likelihood. He wearily climbed over the fence and crawled in the pickup. Jim respected his mood and they drove to Piney Meadows in silence.

It was a five minute ride east to the Meadows. This one was all government. There were some long low buildings that looked like nothing so much as military barracks. Jim explained that some of the bachelor rangers lived there and it was used to house some of the forest service experts that come through on a transient basis while they plied whatever temporary specialty they had. Like some of the other things they'd seen lately, the barracks had seen better days. The sickly green paint was peeling from the cinder block walls in places and the whole place just had a dispirited look to it.

Jim parked in a gravel parking lot and motioned Jasper to follow as he walked toward the end of the building. When they got nearly there, he saw that there was a sign in the window that proclaimed that this was the office of the barracks sergeant. Jim pushed in the open door, hollering. "Harky, whar yu be?"

A large man in the uniform of the forest service turned from where he had been searching in a file drawer. Striding forward, he held his hand out as he bawled, "Jim. Why I ain't seen you for a coons age." He turned a bit more serious as he asked, "You still a runnin' 'round up there in the mountains? Er have ya gone back ta ranchin' so's you can stand me to a drunk now an' agin."

Jim turned a beaming face on Jasper, evidently because of the others recognition of his mountain man status. He clapped the other on a shoulder with enough force to have stunned a bear. "Ah'll stan' ya to a drunk enny tam. Ah ain' acomin' out a ta mountin's though. Them thar comminists ain' gone tell me whut ta do."

This must have been an old argument and the big man shook it off with a chuckle. "Who's your pard?" he asked.

With a wide grin showing his white teeth through the thick beard, Jim turned and introduced Jasper. He introduced the other as Harkness Wilding, with a snorting question as to whether he'd ever heard such a pretentious thing in his life. "We's lookin' fer a strayed hoss. Yu got airy a 'em 'round 'bout?"

Harky stared at Jim much as the chief ranger had earlier done. "You huntin' your own strayed horses now, are ya Jim?"

Jim must have forgotten his earlier embarrassment because he again looked startled. "Uh....Wal, jes this un. It be a kinda special hoss, don' yu know?"

Harky looked definitely interested now. "Special, do ya say? In what way is it special?"

"Wal....It ain' thet it's so special...." Jim was clearly floundering at being called on to explain something that he hadn't in any way anticipated.

Jasper cut in. "It's just that this is a kind a pet, ya know?"

Harky looked bemused. "A pet, did ya say. Ol' Jim's got him a pet hoss." He turned to Jim with an astonished look. "I never thought a you havin' a pet hoss, Jim." He chuckled, which seemed to embarrass Jim mightily. "Well, I'm not sure what it is that we got, but what there is, is out there in the south meadow. If you can wait for a while, I'll go along with you."

Giving Jasper a quick look, Jim hurried to say, "Wal, ol' Harky, ah b'lieve thet we jes go long an see, if it's alrat. Yu come along soon's yo done an' we do some mo' talkin' 'bout dranking an one thang 'nother."

Turning back to his file cabinet, Harky waved a dismissal. "You know where it's at. I'll hurry here, an' be right along."

Chapter Seventeen

The south meadow proved to be just a short way along through some high brush and low trees. Before he got close, Jasper saw her. There were eight horses in the meadow and Genevieve was one of the closest. As they walked to the fence, she threw up her head and saw them. After staring for just a few seconds, she snorted happily and broke into a trot toward them.

Jasper threw his arms around her head and hugged her. "Bettah back off, Friend Jasper. If'n ol' Harky was ta see ya a huggin' thet hoss, it mount mek him 'spicious."

Reluctantly, Jasper backed away. Genevieve clearly didn't like that and responded with a small whinny. She trotted up and down, clearly wanting to get out and go with them. Jasper figured that she'd finally got her fill of being with other horses and was ready to go along with him now.

"We bettah jes git on back ta b'rracks. Be bettah if'n ol' Harky don' be seein' us wif her a tryin' ta git out an go. Mount mek him watch her more'n he ought."

Realizing that Jim was entirely right, Jasper turned and determinedly walked away, although it was one of the hardest things he'd ever done.

They'd nearly got back to the barracks when they met Harky. "That didn't take long. Must not a been there, huh?"

Jim answered with a casual negative. Seeing her had made Jasper preoccupied and he just stood by as the other two bantered back and forth for a few minutes more.

As they got in the pickup, Jasper hastened to ask, "Well, what do ya think? How we gonna do it?"

"Wal, ah do b'lieve it be easy as pie. Thet meadow be most hid by thet high bresh an' them leetle trees. We jes gits oursefs a hoss trailah an' come on back heah arter dark. Be no trouble atall fer yu ta git 'er an' load 'er up. They won' pay much nevah mind if'n we don' mek much tracks. They pro'ly jes thank she got out an' went back ta where evah she done come frum."

Jasper leaned back and took a deep breath. He wanted to believe it would be all that simple. Things hadn't taken a simple turn since he'd lost Genevieve and he had a hard time believing that they might now. There was nothing to do though, except go along. Jim might have it figured out this time. It sounded good anyhow.

By the time they got back to Laran, it was lunch time and past. Jim stopped at a restaurant where he said he was known and would get good food and service. Jasper was so preoccupied that such things were lost on him. He ate, but couldn't have said what it was.

After eating, they drove to one of Jims ranches. He said it was the third one that he'd bought. There, they inspected three trailers parked in a row. There was a very large one that would have hauled several horses and even had a small sleeping room fixed up in the front for the horse handler. They passed that one by with no more than a glance. The last one in the row was obviously disigned to haul just two horses. It appeared to be the one that Jim was interested in. He inspected the tires, grumbling about one of them. Eventually, he pronounced the trailer fit and they hitched it to the pickup and departed for the main ranch house.

It was only midafternoon when they got there and Jasper knew that they couldn't leave until dark. Jim said that he had a couple of matters of business that he'd just as well do since he was down here from the mountains. The suggestion that Jasper take a nap so he'd be fresh for the nights work was a welcome one. He was tired and after Jim left on his errands, he lay down on the bed in his room.

He'd nearly dozed off when visions of what could go wrong began to occur to him. He sat up and thought about it for a few minutes. He'd come so far and had so much trouble that the thought of something unforseen taking his chance to get Genevieve back tonight was unnerving.

He found himself pacing the floor and mumbling to himself. Finally, he left the house and walked down through the field behind it toward the small river.

It was calming to just walk along the murmuring stream. He found himself leaning against a tree and quietly contemplating the future. The accident prone streak that had plagued his life seemed to still be going strong. Witness the things that had happened to him just in the past few weeks. Some of the things that had happened had been precipitated by Jim, but it seemed that the result inevitably came back to him. He seemed to be the beneficiary no matter who did the deed.

He had been about as happy in the moutains with Genevieve as he'd ever been. He guessed that when, or if things worked out tonight, he'd head back there. He'd got used to Jim too. Maybe they could make a team. He didn't seem to mind the things that happened to Jasper. Mostly, he seemed unaware that misfortune seemed to be their constant companion. Yeah, there were things that could be worse than having Jim for a pardner when he went back to the mountains. It would mainly depend on how things went tonight.

Sighing, he turned and began to slowly make his way back toward the house. He noticed that the sun had gone down.

Jim was home and he seemed unconcerned. "Ah looked in on ya, but yu wuzn't 'round. Tek a wak, did ya?"

"Yeah. Guess I was some worried 'bout things goin' right tonight."

Jim had sandwich makings spread out on the table and he was in the process of building a giant concoction. He put off answering for a minute as he wrestled with a giant piece of lettuce. Subduing it, he looked up at Jasper. "Ah c'n unnerstan thet. An they is sho' thangs thet cud go wrong. Seems simple 'nough though. If'n we stikes out t'nat, why we jes tries agin. Whut cud be mo' simpler than thet?"

Jim had a way of cutting right to the bone of the matter that seemed to be just what Jasper with his more complex way of looking at things needed. He thought for only a second before nodding. "What could be more simple. Mind if I build me one a them sandwiches?"

By the time they'd finished eating and had done a bit of cleanup, it was full dark. Looking out the window, Jasper asked when Jim thought they ought to go.

"Why, Ah doubts it gone git enny bettah then this. Le's do it."

They'd no more than got on the road than Jasper knew that his worst nightmare was coming true. They pulled out on the road and went no more than a quarter of a mile before a car came around the curve ahead. Jim, without seeming to realize it at all, began to drift into the other lane. Faced with a headon collision, Jasper tried to squawk a warning, but he was so startled by what Jim was doing that he couldn't utter a sound.

The oncoming car did it for him. Taking to the barditch with a blaring horn and a shaking fist out of the open side window, it passed them.

Jim peered near sightedly into his mirror. "Whut yu reckon thet fool were a honkin' he horn fer?"

Jasper had to try twice to find his voice. "What was he....." He realized he was nearly screaming, and stopped a second while he controled his voice. "Jim, yu 'bout hit that there feller. Didn' ya see 'im?"

Jims voice was deeply disgusted. "Whut yu mean, din' ah see 'im? Sho' an' ah saw 'im. Rat in mah lane, he were. An' then ta honk on me. If'n ah wuz thet kinda a feller, ah'd turn 'roun' an' chase 'im down an' whup on 'im jes a leetle bit."

Jasper was staring at the other with wide eyes. He realized his mouth was hanging open too. He suddenly realized that he should have known this would happen. He'd seen how Jim seemed to be mostly unable to see in dusky or dark conditions. He'd been the beneficiary of Jim taking the wrong direction back in the rangers camp and ending up standing on his hand. The skunk stew when he'd first met the big mountain man. How could he have forgotten those things. He guessed that the only excuse would be that he was so preoccupied with things down here. It just might be a preoccupation that could cost him dearly.

He'd thought about it too long though. As he turned his head back to the front, it was just in time to see the bright headlights and high clearance lights of a big truck. Jim seemed to have again been drawn into the other lane and the truck and their pickup was threatening to mate at a high rate of speed.

"Arrrrrgh......" Jasper screamed as he dropped to the floorboards. He knew that doing that wouldn't protect him from the immenant collision, but it was an automatic protest.

He heard the blaring truck air horn and the pickup swerved. He'd never know how the wreck was avoided. The last thing he'd seen was that there was a concrete retaining wall along the side of the trucks lane. There was just nowhere for the trucker to go.

He was still laying on the floor boards, shaking and shuddering when Jims unperturbed voice asked, "Whut be it thet yu air a lookin' fer, down thar neighbor Jasper?"

Looking up, Jasper still couldn't believe that he was alive and whole. He grabbed the edge of the dash board and pulled hismself up just enough to peek out the windshield. He was just in time to see cars careening on both sides of the pickup as Jim still looked at him with concern. There were more cars ahead, streaking straigt at them and Jasper again dropped to the floorboard and clasping his hands over his head, waited for death.

"Ah reckon ah bettah pull ovah an' let yu git a breaf a air."

It took a moment for what Jim was suggesting to sink in. When it did, he felt like crying with gratitude. He couldn't imagine why he hadn't thought of that himself. "Yes." He cried. "Yes." But until the pickup completely stopped, he kept his arms clasped over his head.

He shakily climbed to the seat and looked around. Jim had pulled off the road into a large parking lot that was right by the now busy street that they'd been on. This parking lot was for the patrons of the large building in the center. There were a number of cars parked around the building itself, but out where they were, it was totally deserted.

He climbed from the pickup and leaned against the side. He felt like throwing up, but after a couple of deep breaths, controlled that urge.

Jim came around the pickup and asked with a deeply concerned voice, "Whut be it thet's wrong, Friend Jasper? Yu reckon thet it be a bit a bad meat thet were in thet thar sammich?"

Jasper looked at him. It was nearly beyond his belief that Jim didn't know how close he'd come to disaster. "Jim, didn' you see how close you came to hittin' them there fellers?" He gestured toward the highway.

Jims voice was indignant. "Wal, ah knows thet them thar fellers is some short a knowin' 'bout dravin'." He shook his head with the disgust that his next remark betrayed. "Thar they be, rat out on ta road, an gittin' in ta wrong place. Mekin' us nervous and bein' dang'rous ta boot. But they is allas thar. Ya cain' let yusef git so upset 'bout these heah leetle thangs." He advised Jasper.

Feeling a bit stronger, Jasper looked around. "What is that place anyhow?" He indicated the building in the center of the parking lot where they were.

Peering that way, Jim seemed unsure. He muttered something about it being this or that. About that time Jasper spotted a sign and shared it with Jim. "It says it's the Golden West Bar."

"Oh yeah. Ta Gold'n West. Ah knowed thet. It were jes worry 'bout yu thet hed me confused fer jes a bit." Jims voice was dismissive. "Wal if'n yu feels lak it, whut yu say le's go on?"

Jasper straightened at that suggestion. One of the few things he was sure of was that he wasn't ready to get back out on that road with Jim driving. "Uh Jim, you reckon maybe I could try drivin'? I sure would admire to drive one a these new pickups."

Jim peered at him. "Ah don' know, friend Jasper. Yu sho' yu know 'bout dravin' this yere fo' wheel drave pickup?"

Jasper was sure that he'd never driven anything like a four wheel drive. He was also sure that he wasn't going to tell Jim any such thing. "Why sure. I believe that I can drive it all right." He started to move around to the drivers side.

"Oh, ah cudn' let ya drave tanat. Why, yu know yo' ownse'f thet thars crazy dravers out thar. Need a steady an' 'sperianced hand on ta wheel. Ah'll let ya drave tomorrer though, yu bet. Yu git used ta draving, yu c'n have a pickup ta drave ever whar."

Jasper opened his mouth to protest. Then he closed it. This was Jims pickup after all. He had no right to protest him driving it. He was becoming desperate though. He knew that he needed Jims help. Had to have it, in fact. But if they went back out on the road, they were taking their lives in their hands. Looking around for inspiration, he spied the Golden West Bar. It suddenly seemed like salvation to him. At least temporary salvation.

"Jim, I do feel a bit shaky. What do ya say we get ourselves a drink 'fore we go?"

Jim peered doubtfully toward the bar. "Wal, ah don' know. We gots ta be gittin' 'bout our b'iness, don' yu reckon?" The last part of this statement seemed to be getting weaker and it was immediately followed by, "But come ta thank on it, why a leetle drank'ud set us rat up. Yu rat, friend Jasper. Le's jes git rat in thar an' have ourse'fs a bit a cheer."

Grabbing Jasper by the arm, he dragged him toward the building as though he thought he might change his mind. And that was something that Jasper was about to do. He'd no more than made the suggestion than the thought intruded, of having to resume the trip with a drunken as well as nearly blind Jim. The very thought made him feel weak at the knees. The only thing that made him remain silent was the immediate spectre of climbing in the pickup to resume the trip. He chose the cowardly way out, hoping that maybe something more attractive would come along.

Jasper was little interested in the interior of the place, but he did notice that it was an enormous room. There was a long bar along one wall and there were probably fifty tables scattered throughout the room. In addition, there were probably about twenty booths along two of the remaining walls. The remaining wall was given over to a stage for a live band which was not now in attendance. Between the tables and the stage was a small bare area for dancing. Although there was a juke box loudly playing, the dance floor was deserted.

There weren't many people here tonight. Five or six tables had patrons at them, mostly men and women leaning close in the dim lighting. There were a dozen patrons at the bar and as Jim approached them, it appeared that he must have known at least most of them. He greeted them loudly and received enthusiastic replies in return.

He moved to the end and clapping the man sitting there on the shoulder with one hand as he slapped the bar with the other, he hollered to the grinning bartender, "A round fer ta house."

This predictably brought cheers and as the bartender busied himself, Jim began to move down the bar with a word for eveyrone, joking and laughing. Jasper settled on a stool and contemplated his future. For the first time in a long time, the dim part wasn't all concerned with getting Genevieve back. In fact, he'd forgotten her entirely in the prospects of his own immediate mortality.

About then, the bartender moved up and asked what he wanted. He distractedly ordered a shot of bar whiskey. He really didn't think about it but he was still shaky and felt that he needed something to brace him.

When it came, he slugged it down and barely felt the burn. He nodded when asked about a refill and he slugged it down when it came. The bartender got busy after that for a few minutes and as he waited, he found that he was feeling easier.

When the bartender came back this time, he ordered a mixed drink and moved back to a table where he reclined into a chair and watched Jim circulate.

He was on his third mixed drink when Jim finally came back and slumped in a chair on the opposite side of the table. His eyes were bright behind the thick glasses. "Yu adoin' alrat, neighbor Jasper?"

"Fine as twine." Quipped a mellow Jasper. His lips felt numb and he wasn't sure that he was articulating clearly, but Jim didn't seem to notice. He'd also completely forgotten that he would have to face the dangerous street sometime later.

Jim stared at him for a second, nonplussed. Then he erupted in laughter. "Fan as twan. Fan as twan. Thet be a fan joke, friend Jasper."

Jasper chuckled along weakly, wishing Jim wouldn't be so loud about it. Even in his mellow condition, he knew the small quip wasn't so funny as all that. It was obvious that Jim was feeling good though and Jasper saw no reason to lessen his enjoyment at all. The numb feeling in his lips was of concern to him however. He wasn't drunk enough to have forgotten why they were out here tonight. He figured that much more to drink might very well be too much. "Jim, don' ya reckon we oughta get goin'. We've had a bit to drink an' much more might get to us."

Jim looked thoughtful. "Wal, ah'm ahavin' rat much fun heah. But, ah knows yo' rat." He gave it another moments thought before announcing regretfully, "Yeah, we bettah move 'long alrat."

He heaved himself to his feet and started for the door with Jasper following closely. They were nearly there when a tall skinny man wearing an enormous cowboy hat entered. Jim stopped as though he'd run into a wall. Throwing his arms wide he bawled, "Anson, whar 'bouts yu been?"

Anson, whoever he was, avoided the embrace and danced around throwing mock punches. "Homer, are you abuyin' ta night?"

It was evidence of their closeness that Jim didn't seem to notice the use of his former name. "Why, ah sho....." He caught sight of Jasper right then and evidently remembered what they'd been doing.

"Ah....Jasper, this heah be Anson Peterson. He an ol' pard a mine." He leaned close and whispered, "Ah jes gotta hev a drank wif ol' Anson. We go rat 'long, afta."

Jasper knew that there was probably no way around it. He gave in with good grace. "Le's sit down right here, how 'bout it?"

They sat down at a table that was vacant just behind them. After getting a drink, Jasper tried to follow the banter of the other two, but he found his attention drifting.

Three drinks later, he took stock. Even his teeth seemed numb now. He knew that they'd better leave now or they wouldn't do it tonight. "Jim, we don' go now, I don' reckon we gonna be able to go."

Jim turned and blearily regarded him. "Ah knows yu rat, friend Jasper." Turning back to Anson to say so long, he took a last sip and stood. Jasper joined him and clinging to each others arms, they made their way to the door and outside.

Jasper stood and breathed deep of the cool night air. It seemed to brace him but it also made him aware of just how wobbly he was.

"Wal, le's git at it." Jim launched a course for the pickup that was barely visible in the distance and the dark. As he stepped off the curb to the parking lot level, he fell full length. Hurrying to help him, Jasper took his own fall. Neither was hurt and they laughingly helped each other up and keeping a hold on each other to steady the staggers, they arrived at the pickup.

As Jasper crawled inside, he had a moments disquiet. He knew there was something that he'd been worried about but he couldn't dredge it up through the alchoholic fog that swirled in his brain.

Jim had climbed into the drivers side and started the pickup, but he wasn't going anywhere. He was just sitting there staring straight ahead. "Somepin wrong, Jim?"

Jim turned an owlish look on him. "Yu reckon as how yu 'member whut it be thet we wuz a gunna do, neighbor Jasper. Seems lak ah disremember."

Even through the fog in his mind, Jasper remembered that they were supposed to be going after Genevieve. "Why, we goin' to get my horse at the rangers. You 'member don' ya?"

Jim slapped his knee. "Why, how cud ah have fergot. Sho' an' thet's whut we is doin'. An we gonna git 'bout doin' it rat now too."

He put the pickup in gear and pulled out into traffic. As he pulled into the traffic lane, he barely missed an oncoming car and that jarred Jaspers memory. The whole thing came flooding back and he remembered all of it. Why they'd gone into the bar and the fear that he'd had about the drunken Jim.

He swung his gaze to the road and sure enough, there was a pair of headlights coming that looked as though they couldn't miss hitting the pickup headon.

With a piteous groan, Jasper slid to the floor boards and covered his head with his arms. There, he waited patiently for death. The wait was too long though. In two seconds flat, he was asleep.

Chapter Eighteen

The pickup hitting a big bump of some kind and tossing Jasper up against the bottom of the dash woke him. There was the noise of the pickup squeaking and banging over large bumps. There were also other noises, the snapping of breaking branches and the screeching of limbs scratching their way down the side of the vehicle.

This lasted only a few seconds and then the pickup stopped and silence came. Jasper picked himself up and took stock. Except for a few sore places, he seemed to be alright. He looked over at Jim to see if he was alright but he had opened his door and was in the process of getting out.

Jasper checked his own door and it opened with only a little effort against the obstruction of the broken branches that pressed against it on the outside. He felt definitely wobbly when he got out and he had to hold to the pickup as he made his way to the front to join Jim.

The pickup had broken through a hedge or at least some thick growth of bushes and small trees. Here in front though, the nose of the vehicle was through into the clear and there was no more growth, just lush grass.

Jasper looked around and saw in the near distance some lights that looked blurred. After blinking several times without clearing the picture of what he was seeing, he gave it up and acknowledged that his sight was affected by what he'd drunk. He turned to Jim and asked, "Where at you reckon we are, Jim?"

Jim had been staring at the pickup where it had emerged from the thick growth. Now, he turned and looked vaguely around. "Ah 'spects it mus' be at ta meadow."

"Oh, the meadow." Jasper nodded and looked around again. He felt pretty weak and guessed he'd better get after finding Genevieve if he was ever going to.

Just then, Jim slumped to the grass. "You ok, Jim?" Jasper asked solicitously.

"Yeah, ah am. ah'm purty tared though. Ah thank we orta rest a bit."

"Well, but......" Jasper knew he ought to argue for an immediate foray after Genevieve. He sat down so as to be able to argue on the same level as Jim was. But the grass was so soft and anyway Jim wasn't at that level anymore. He'd now reclined full length and not only that, he was sonorously snoring. Jasper shrugged and lay down himself. Maybe it was better that they rest just a little.

Someone was shaking him and he came up fighting because the shaking was threatening to dislodge his head from his shoulders. "Whut......What is it you want?" His voice came out no more than a croak.

Someone jerked him to his feet and he looked wildly around. It was full light although the sun had yet to come up. The light that was there though seemed to lance into his eyes and made his head explode into a pain that made him squint and groan.

He turned his squint on the man who had him by the arm and was surprised to see that he wore the star of a deputy sheriff. He was also holding Jaspers wallet. Jasper tried to pull himself to his full height, a manuever that was somewhat spoiled by his wobbly condition. "What's the trouble?" He asked in that voice that seemed to resemble nothing he'd ever heard before.

The man chuckled as he handed the wallet back to Jasper. He'd evidently looked at his drivers licence, since he now called him by name. "Well mister Caine, there's enough wrong to go around." He nodded behind Jasper to where the pickup was nestled. Jaspers gaze narrowed even more as he looked at the pickup. He seemed to remember something about the episode but it was like a hazy dream. He switched his attention to the side where Jim was being held by another deputy. Jims face looked swelled and he was squinting through the thick glasses as if he just couldn't believe whatever it was that he was seeing.

Deciding there was no point in asking Jim anything in his present shape, he looked around to try see if he could get any clue as to their exact location. Full twenty twenty vision had returned, although hindered by a bad headache. The sign on the building that had been behind him and that he now faced was the same one that he'd seen the other day. It was the one that said `Headquarters, Hiute Forestry District.'

His mouth fell open. He spun and looked at Jim. "Jim, This here's ranger headquarters. What are we doin' here?"

Jims head swiveled owlishly. "Ah don' know friend Jasper. Ah thought ah wuz agoin' ta meadow. Musta took a wrong turn. Er mebbe ah misunderstood whar we wuz 'sposed ta be goin'." His voice was thoroughly miserable and apologetic.

Jasper shrugged it off. The most likely thing that occured to him was that it was just as Jim suggested. In their drunken state, Jim must have automatically brought them to ranger headquarters, which was where they'd first gone the other day. He looked around helplessly. Suddenly, it seemed all too much. No matter what he'd tried to do, things had gone irrivocably wrong. It seemed too much.

He turned to the deputy. "I want to confess."

The deputy gave his comrade a small smirk. "Well, ya don't really got to confess." He nodded to the pickup and the broken and smashed bushes. "Seems like we kinda got you in the act, so to speak. I don' really b'lieve you gotta go to the trouble to confess."

Jasper tried to brush that off with a gesture. "Not this. I gotta confess 'bout something else."

This earthshaking news seemed to interest them a little, but not all that much. "Well, we're ready to take you down to headquarters anyhow. If you wanta confess, save it for the captain."

Both were still shaky to the point of needing help to get into the cramped back seat of the patrol car.

Inside the sherrifs office, Jasper was more than happy to be able to slump into a chair. Jim took a chair of his own and then silently stared at the floor.

They'd sat there for about twenty minutes before a rather small and thin man came out. He wore the same uniform as the others, but he had two silver bars on his collar. In spite of feeling about as depressed as he'd ever remembered feeling, Jasper had very nearly drifted off to sleep.

"Mister Caine, I understand that you want to talk to me."

Jasper had to clear his throat before he could make a sound. "Uh yeah. I want to confess."

The officer gave him a level stare and then transferred the look to Jim, who'd looked up briefly before again taking up his study of the floor. Turning back to Jasper, he said, "Well, come on in. We'll see what you got on your mind."

There was a desk inside with a couple of chairs in front of it. Jasper took one of them and waited as the captain got a yellow tablet and wrote along the top. When he finished, he regarded Jasper and said only, "Shoot."

"Bout two months ago, more er less, I stole an ol' pickup with a horse trailer an' a horse. It was up in La Junta."

The captain wrote for a minute before leaning back in his chair and regarding Jasper gravely. "What's the reason you come in here now and tell us about that?"

Jasper shrugged miserably. "I don't know. After all thats happened, I just seem to have got disgusted with the whole thing. I had her, that is the horse, up in the mountains. She got in with a couple of rangers livestock and no matter how I tried, I just couldn't get her back. They came on down here and we, that's me and Jim.... Uh, I guess you'd call him Homer. Anyhow, we had this scheme to kinda steal her back. Didn't go any better than the other things I tried. After gettin' arrested this morning, I kinda lost hope. I just don't wanta be lookin' over my shoulder no more."

The captain leaned back and scratched his head as he regarded Jasper curiously. "Ya know, La Junta is the neighboring county over northeast a here. We share all of the bulletins and wanted posters on men, an' property too." He shifted his gaze to the ceiling for a minute before looking back at Jasper. "Trouble is, there hasn't been any pickups and trailers stole for a while. Sure not in the past few months. Well, 'cept for the ol' Bindle boys, at least. I know for a fact that they was the only ones that stole any pickup an' trailer thats been stole for a while."

"Well, I don't know about no Bindle boys. I come on that pickup an' trailer outside of a cafe up to the west side of La Junta. That's where I took it from. Are you sayin' that nobody reported it stolen?"

The captain was again staring at Jasper intently. "Ya know, you're kinda telling a story a lot like the Bindle boys told it. They said they was in a cafe up to the west end of La Junta and somebody come in and stole the pickup and trailer that they'd already stole. Course, no body believed them. It was kinda funny though that they didn't never deny stealing the thing. They just seemed to be mad that some body stole it from them. They got a trial comin' up here in a couple of weeks. I figure them two will get life at least."

Jasper looked at him with wide eyes. "They gonna get life for stealing a pickup an' trailer?"

The captain waved a deprecating hand. "Naw, I didn't mean that. I only brought up the pickup and trailer stealing charge because of what you said. That's the least of the charges against them. They robbed a store here and shot the cashier. He didn't die, but they got about every assault charge in the books against them. And then there's an arson charge over in Lamar. If we ever get through with them here, they'll get their turn over there." He thought a minute. "This does intrigue me though. You say that you stole that pickup and trailer in La Junta. What did you do with it?"

"I took it to a campground on the eastern edge of the Hiute Wilderness Area. Glen Creek Campground, I think it was."

Again the captian took a moment to think before slowly shaking his head. "It's a mighty interesting story. Only thing is, you're the only one that's ever said anything about a horse. The Beasly ranch over by Walsenburg where the boys stole the rig only reported a rig stole. The Bindle boys never said a word about a horse. If it wasn't for that, I might just believe what you say."

Jasper shook his head tiredly. "Well, I just wanted to do the right thing. Like I said, I got tired a lookin' over my shoulder."

The captain leaned forward. "Look, let's just say that there's something to what you been tellin' me. We already done a heap of investigation into the Bindle boys. The rig stealin' charge is just a little thing among all the rest, but if we have to change it now, it just might throw the whole case out of joint. If there's anything to what you say, you only stole what had already been stole an' then you didn't keep it. There doesn't seem to be anything at all against you for the horse. I say, go on your way. Let things lay as they are. What do you say?"

Jasper rose. "I was sorry I started the whole thing before I even got here. You'll never see nobody any happier to forget it either. Goodbye captain." His last sight of the other was the captain leaning forward on his desk with a sharp speculative look in his eye.

Jim was still sitting and glumly regarding the floor. "Jim, what we gotta do about running through them bushes. Can we just pay a fine and get on out of here."

Jim looked up at him. "Did yu tell 'em 'bout thangs. Ah'm awful sorry thet ah got us in ta pickle."

Jasper shrugged. "They didn't believe me. Jim, I just want to get on out of here. Did they tell you anything that we gotta do?"

Jim shrugged. "Yeah. Rangah Long were in heah laughin' lak a fool. He knows ah'll pay 'im fer ennythang thets broke, but he had ta come an' needle me a bit. We c'n go enny tam we want."

One of the departing patrol cars gave them a ride back to the ranger headquarters. Both were frowning and disgusted with the laughter of the departing patrolman echoing in their ears as he drove off.

In the full light of the sun, the devastation caused by the pickup and trailer plowing through the beautiful shrubbery was even worse than Jasper had remembered.

One thing he hadn't noticed this morning was that in bouncing high over the curb, the horse trailer had come loose and had plowed a small furrow of it's own that was separate from the pickup. It sat a few feet to the side forlornly draped in broken branches. There were a few rangers standing on the lawn laughing and cutting up. That alone seemed to make the whole thing worse.

Jim sighed. "Wal, we jes as well git at it. Ah sho' do hate this yere whole thang." He shook his hairy head at the injustice of the world as he pushed his way through the tangled and broken growth to the pickup.

Twenty minutes later, they'd accomplished it. There was even more devastation in the foliage now, as they'd had to back in over previously undisturbed growth to hook on the trailer. Their activities had drawn quite a crowd of onlookers too. All this was most unappreciated by the two hungover workers. They persevered though, and completed everything in a wounded silence.

Just as soon as they regained the street, Jim accelerated away. He, especially had seemed to chaff under the onlookers banter that had accompanied their efforts to get the pickup and trailer remated and moving.

Several blocks away, they came to a cafe and Jim pulled in. Turning to Jasper, he said, "Ah jes cain go enny mo' wifout a bit a coffee ta perk me up. What ya say, friend Jasper?"

Jasper had been in his own blue funk and right now nothing had ever sounded quite so good. He gave an enthusiastic nod and they proceeded inside.

Nothing at all was said until they'd received and tasted their coffee. As they drank the rest, Jasper finally came to a point in his thinking. "Jim, I been havin' a bit of trouble trying to think this out. This here hangover ain't helpin'. An' then, while we was gettin' the pickup out, I was just wanting to get gone away from those hecklers. But listen, does this sound right to you. If the sheriffs department don' think I stole Genevieve, why couldn't we just go out and claim her?"

Jim was staring at Jasper as though he'd never seen him before. "Whoa. Whut is it thet yu mean thet ta sh'rf don' thank yu stole thet hoss? Why'nt they think that? Whut wuz it thet yu tolt 'em?"

"Well, to answer your questions in reverse. I told 'em that I'd stole Genevieve. Along with the pickup an' trailer, of course. He said that they'd already got the fellers that had stole the pickup an' trailer. The Bindle boys, he called them. You ever heard of them Bindle boys?"

"Yeah, ah hev. Them there boys is beena roustin' an' a rompin' 'round 'bout this whole country fer quite a spell. So they finally got somepin on them boys, did they?" This last was said musingly, almost to himself.

"Well, I guess they got 'em for most everything in the books. Thing is though, according to the captain over in the sheriffs office, nobody at all ever reported a horse stolen. An' since they already got the Bindle boys for stealing the pickup and trailer, they don't really want me fouling up the works by claiming I stole that rig from the boys, since it was the boys that stole it originally,"

This last seemed to be a bit much for Jim, whose eyes behind the thick glasses seemed just a little glassy. He shook off the part that he didn't understand though. "Wal, if it be thet nobody has reported her stole, it seems ta me lak yu rat. Ol' Harky pro'ly won' ask much questions ennyhow. Le's drank up and git on out there." The stimulous of again maybe being able to put something over on the forest service had seemed to revitalize Jim.

Twenty minutes later, they were leaning on the fence of the meadow talking to Harky. Jim was off into a lengthy story explaining why he hadn't recognized his horse yesterday. Jasper was petting Genevieve, who was snorting with pleasure.

After just a bit of this, Harky waved his hand. "Jim, if you can't recognize your own horse, I don't wanta hear about it. Come on in an' sign the papers and get on out of here. I got work to do." They moved off to the office with Harky loudly proclaiming the debt of a huge drunk that Jim would owe him for all this paper work.

There was a gate a short way to the south and Jasper got a short rope hackamore from the trailer and opening the gate, he put it on Geneveive. She was well used to horse trailers, and stepped up in as though she actually had missed not being in one for a while.

Jim seemed surprised when he came back and found her loaded and ready to go, but he said nothing except to ask if Jasper was all ready to go. Replying in the affirmative, Jasper climbed in.

They were only a couple of blocks into their journey when Jim hesitantly asked, "Whut be it thet yu a gonna do now, neighbor Jasper?"

Faced with the immediacy of some kind of decision, Jasper found he was strangely reluctant to make a decision. This chase had seemed to go for so long that he guessed that at some points, he'd thought it would never end. He'd had some thought, of course, about just going back to the mountains and resuming his mountain man life. For some reason, this didn't now have all the appeal it once had and he didn't know why.

He knew that he had to make a decision though. "I guess I'll just go back to the mountains with Genevieve. Don't seem like there's anything else to do."

Jim didn't look at him as he softly asked, "Wud yu be awantin airy company?"

Suddenly Jasper knew why the prospect of returning to the mountains had lost some of its appeal. It was because in the back of his mind he'd thought that Jim and him had come to the parting of the ways. That thought, although suppressed under the anxieties of the last couple of days, had been there and with the culmination of this little adventure, had surfaced to the point of making him miserable.

He turned to Jim with a great smile. "Would I be wantin' company? You bet I would Jim. That'd make everything right. I thought maybe you wouldn't want to go back with us after all the trouble we been."

Jim turned to face Jasper with a grin of his own. "Ah be rat grateful yu awantin' me, friend Jasper."

With Jim facing him, Jasper turned in alarm to see what was coming down the road. Jim had strayed over about half way into the other lane and an oncoming car was forced to take to the barditch to avoid him. It passed with blaring horn and the drivers shaking fist.

"Durn crazy dravers." Jim declared with a disgusted look.

Jasper grinned. What ever the future held, it wouldn't be dull with Jim around.